THE KID WHO
INVENTED THE
TRAMPOLINE

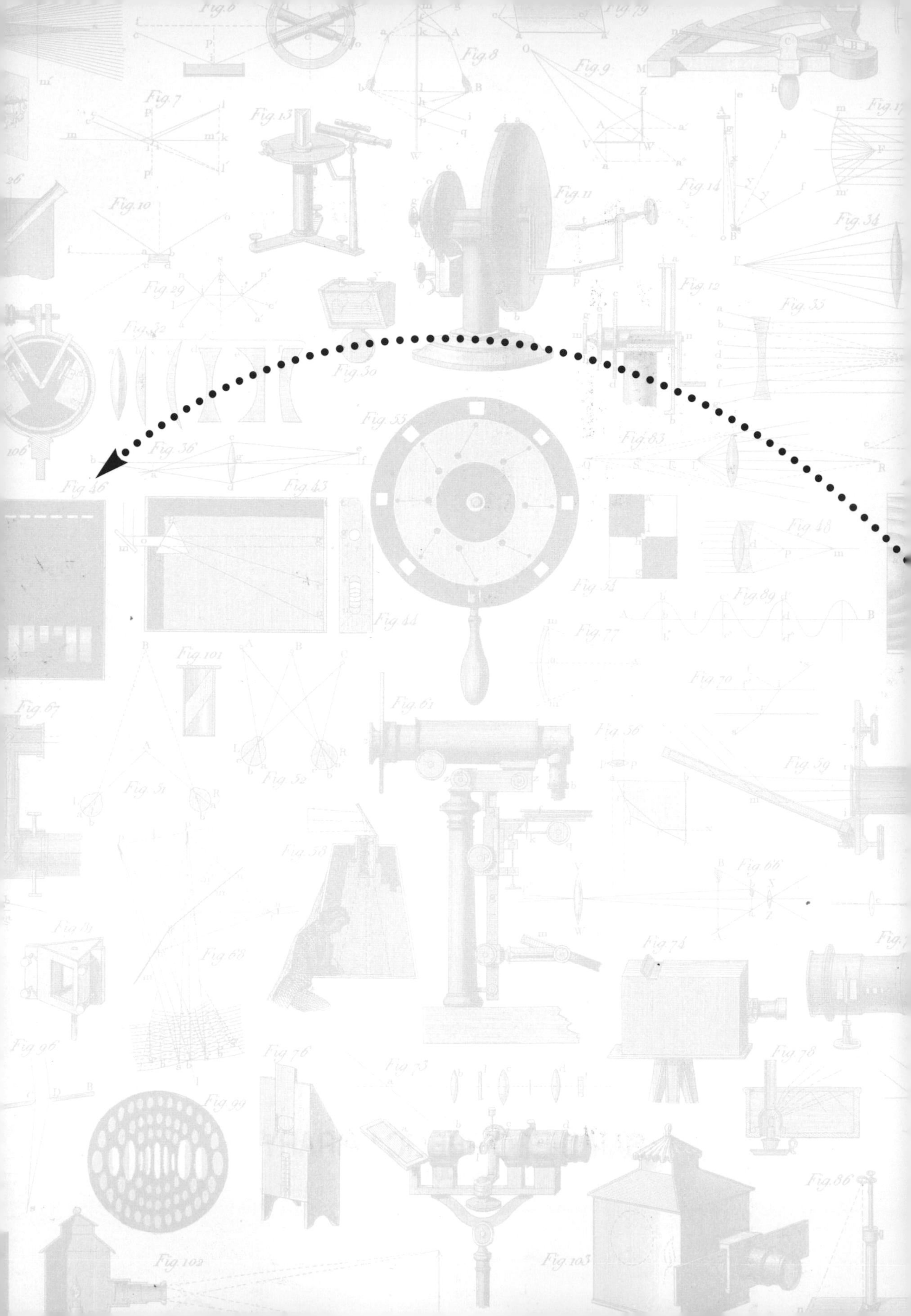

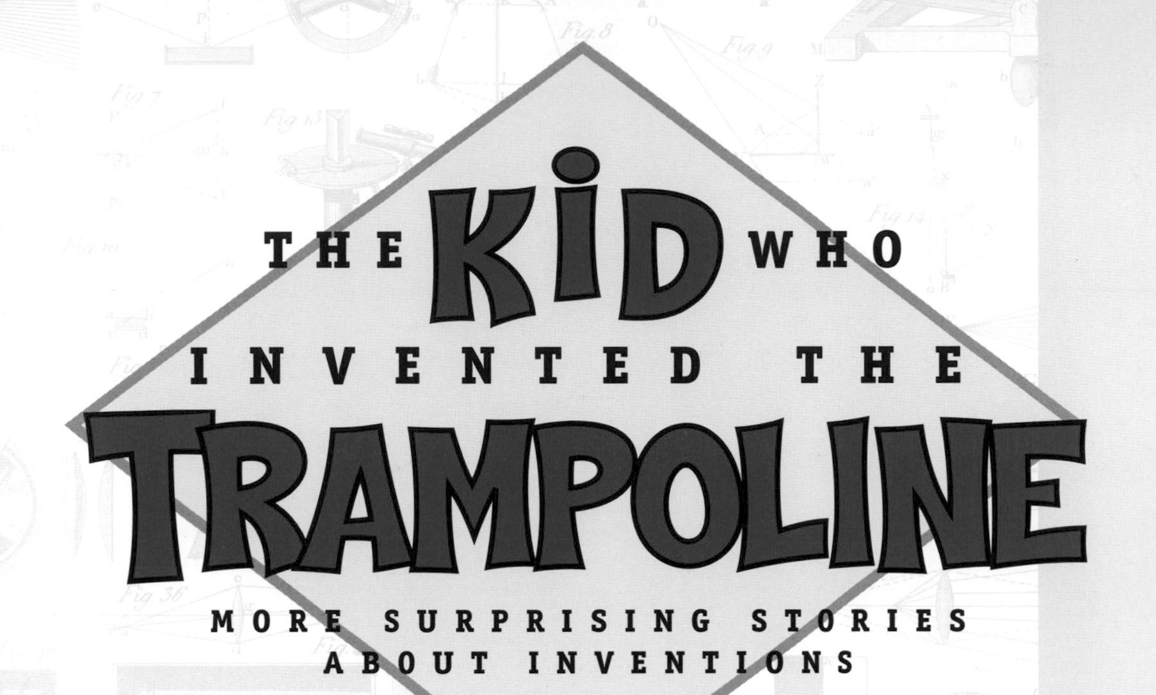

THE KID WHO INVENTED THE TRAMPOLINE

MORE SURPRISING STORIES ABOUT INVENTIONS

by
Don L. Wulffson

Dutton Children's Books • New York

Photo/Illustration Credits: front cover, back cover, p. 100: photos of trampoline exhibition and George Nissen with a kangaroo used by kind permission of George Nissen; front cover, p. 37: photo of George Washington's false teeth courtesy of National Museum of Dentistry, Baltimore, Maryland; back cover, p. 22: photos of cameras from Chris Eve's Kodak Camera Collection, *http://www.toptown.com/nowhere/kypfer/*; back cover, pp. 59, 60: parking meter photos reproduced courtesy of POM Inc.; back cover, p. 64: photo of Arthur Fry reprinted with the permission of 3M; p. 5: the first frame of *Steamboat Willie* used by permission of Disney Enterprises, Inc. © Disney Enterprises, Inc.; pp. 10, 12, 14: photos of glass eye, baby bottles, and silver nipple used by permission of the Mütter Museum, College of Physicians of Philadelphia; p. 16: birthday party photo by Joseph Byron, courtesy of the Museum of the City of New York, The Byron Collection; p. 17: engraving of blood transfusion from *A Pictorial History of Medicine,* 1956, by Otto L. Bettmann, PhD. Courtesy of Charles C. Thomas, Publisher, Ltd., Springfield, Illinois; p. 18: photo of blood transfusion kit used by permission of the Mütter Museum, College of Physicians of Philadelphia; p. 33: original Chux advertisement courtesy of Johnson & Johnson; p. 41: graham cracker advertisement reproduced by permission of Nabisco; p. 44: from *Guinness Book of World Records* (jacket cover), © 2000. Used by permission of Bantam Books, a division of Random House, Inc.; p. 46: Advertisement and slogans are used with permission of Clairol Inc. © 2000 Clairol Inc.; p. 48: advertisement for Heinz tomato ketchup reprinted by permission of H.J.Heinz Company; p. 51: advertisement for Liquid Paper® reprinted by permission of The Gillette Company; p. 56: advertisement for Delrich Margarine reprinted by permission of FNC Holdings Inc. (formerly General Host Corporation); p. 62: photo of Chester F. Carlson courtesy of Xerox Corporation, Xerox Historical Archives, Webster, New York; pp. 69, 70: photos of riders Kari and Shaun White courtesy of Burton Snowboards; p. 72: photo of prototype snowmobile courtesy of Musée J. Armand Bombardier; p. 77: Advertisement for leg makeup from *Everyday Fashions of the Forties as Pictured in Sears Catalogs,* Dover Publications Inc., 1992, is reprinted by arrangement with Sears, Roebuck and Co. and is protected under copyright. No duplication is permitted; p. 79: photo of Tom Blake courtesy Thomas Edward Blake/NGS Image Collection; p. 86: photo of John Logie Baird from the Hulton Getty Collection, used by permission of Liaison Agency Inc., New York; p. 87: advertisement used by permission of Continental General Tire, Inc.; p. 93: photo of toilet papers from the private collection of Gretchen Worden, used by permission; pp. 95, 97: photos of "toothbrush twig" and tooth powder tin courtesy of National Museum of Dentistry, Baltimore, Maryland; pp. 104, 105: The VASELINE petroleum jelly and hair tonic print ads were produced courtesy of Chesebrough-Pond's USA Co., and used with permission; pp. 107, 109: photos courtesy of The National Automatic Merchandising Association; p. 108: photo used by permission of Grand Union Co.; p. 111: photo of the VERA VCR used by permission of the BBC Picture Archives; p. 116: photo by S. Newman Darby © 1964 by S. Newman Darby, used by permission of Naomi Albrecht and S. Newman Darby; pp. 118, 119: photo of Sonja Henie and the ZAMBONI graphic © Frank J. Zamboni & Co., Inc. Used by permission.

Library of Congress Cataloging-in-Publication Data
Wulffson, Don L. • The kid who invented the trampoline:
more surprising stories about inventions / by Don Wulffson.—1st ed.
p. cm. • ISBN 0-525-46654-1 • 1. Inventions—History. I. Title.
T15.W86 2001 609—dc21 00-041699

Published in the United States 2001 by Dutton Children's Books, a division of Penguin Putnam Books for Young Readers, 345 Hudson Street, New York, New York 10014, www.penguinputnam.com
Designed by Richard Amari and Ellen M. Lucaire • Printed in Hong Kong • First Edition
1 3 5 7 9 10 8 6 4 2

To my editors, especially
Meredith Mundy Wasinger,
whose intelligence, vision, and
tireless enthusiasm contributed
so greatly to this book

ACKNOWLEDGMENTS

My sincere thanks to Richard Amari and Laurin Lucaire for their splendid design; to Jennifer Mattson and Cathy Mundy for helping me track down just the right images to accompany each invention; and to Diane Giddis for her eagle-eyed fact-checking expertise. And, most of all, my thanks to my wife, Pam—for everything.

CONTENTS

THE KID WHO
INVENTED THE
TRAMPOLINE

Introduction

"Everything that can be invented has been invented."
—Charles H. Duell, director of the Office of Patents, 1899

The first dentures were made with teeth taken from corpses. Before Charles Goodyear invented a process he called vulcanization, rubber boots smelled so bad they had to be buried underground during the summer. And then there's the baby bottle: the first-ever was made from a dried cow udder! Later came glass bottles with long feeding tubes; they sound like a better, safer invention—but the things were known as "murder bottles," and for good reason.

This is the story of humankind's inventiveness, the story of our endless efforts to make newer and better things. It is a mixed story of success and failure.

Some inventions, like the telescope, were accidents. Most, however, came about as a result of long, tireless quests by brilliant people—sometimes working together—to invent "the impossible." They were the product of cleverness mixed with luck, of sudden inspiration followed by years of hard work.

The last millennium was arguably the most inventive era in human history. But as long as we continue to change the way we live and work, there will always be room for new inventions—marvels we have yet to think of, yet to create.

DON L. WULFFSON

1

Animated Cartoon

In 1877, Frenchman E. Reynaud created a device that, using mirrors and lanterns, projected moving cartoon drawings on a screen.

It was a bright summer day a long time ago—in 1908. A seven-year-old boy was out hiking near his family's farm in Missouri. Suddenly, his eyes grew wide. He'd spotted an owl sleeping on a low branch of a tree. Fascinated, he crept closer to the bird. Then, in a moment of impulsiveness, he tried to capture it with his hands. The bird struggled wildly. The boy, suddenly frantic and frightened, found himself fighting the owl—and accidentally killed it. Sickened by what he had done, the boy vowed never again to hurt an animal. Instead, he would devote his life to drawing them in cartoon form, capturing only their beauty and innocence.

The boy's name was Walt Disney.

At the age of sixteen, Walt went to art school in Chicago. He also worked for a company making short animated advertising films that were shown in local movie theaters. But Walt was restless. He wanted to make truly great animated films—cartoons that showed animals in the happiest, funniest, most wonderful way ever. True, others had made cartoons before him. The first modern cartoon was *Humorous Phases of Funny Faces* in 1906. After that came *The Katzenjammer Kids* in 1916 and *Mutt and Jeff* in 1917. But these early efforts were primitive: the films were very short; they were in black-and-white;

they did not tell a story; and the characters were often "stick people" who didn't speak. Walt Disney knew he could do better—and on all counts, he eventually did.

In 1923, in pursuit of his dream of becoming an animator, Walt took a train from Chicago to Los Angeles. His traveling companion—who lived in his pocket—was a pet mouse he'd named Mortimer. While playing with his pet, Walt suddenly had an idea for a cartoon—one in which the main character was a funny little mouse who talked in a high, squeaky voice and who was always going off on wacky adventures. Naturally, the cartoon mouse would have the same name as his pet: Mortimer Mouse.

Before cartoons on film, there were "peep show" cartoons, found in arcades in the late nineteenth and early twentieth centuries. For a penny, the viewer looked through a slot at a lit-up stack of cards. Turning a crank flipped the cards so fast that they created the illusion of motion.

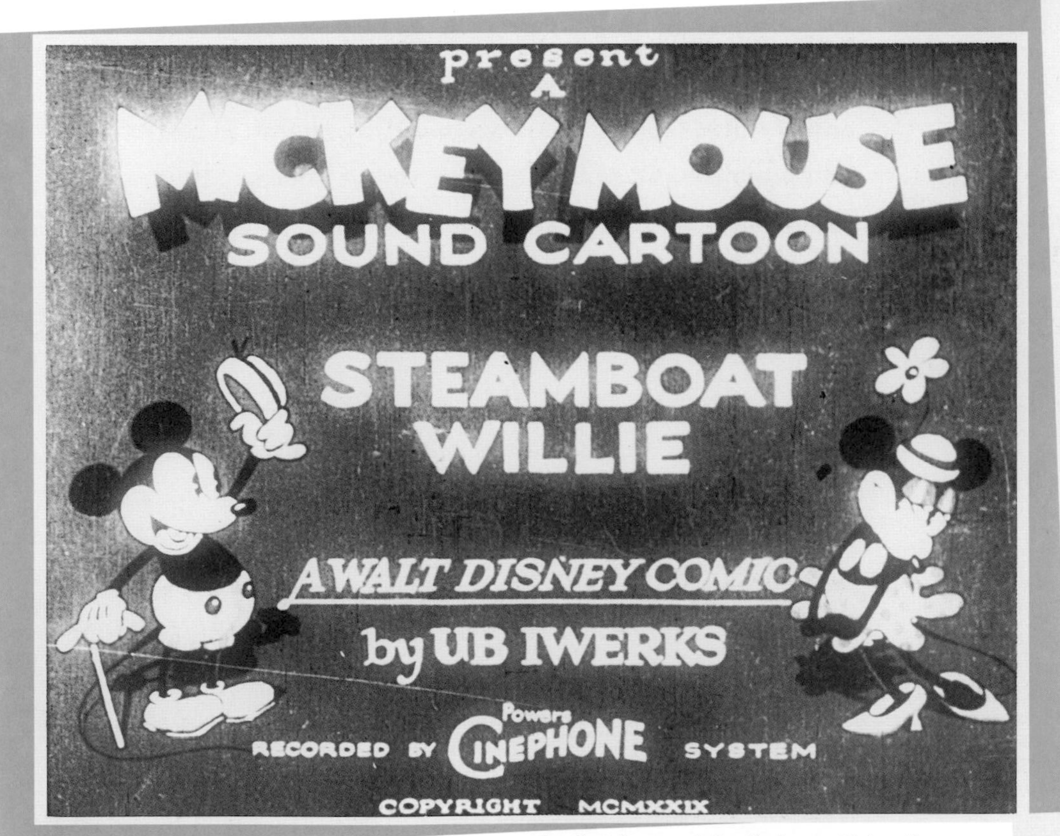

The first frame of the first-ever Mickey Mouse cartoon. ©Disney Enterprises, Inc.

When he was in the fifth grade, Walt Disney memorized the Gettysburg Address, came to school dressed as Lincoln, and performed for every class in the school.

Walt Disney was an ambulance driver in France during World War I (1914–1918).

In 1932, a Mickey Mouse cartoon was banned as obscene in Boston! The cartoon showed a cow reading a book by Elinor Glyn entitled *Three Weeks*. The work, which is about a romance between an Englishman and a Russian queen, had been banned in Boston in 1908 and was considered vulgar by moralists and critics alike. Most likely, a Disney animator with a wacky sense of humor put the book in the cartoon cow's hands.

In Los Angeles, Walt set up his "artist's studio" in a small office. There he and other artists working for him began drawing Mortimer Mouse cartoons. Unlike today, when most cartoons are computer-generated, hundreds of pictures had to be drawn to create just one very short "moving picture." Lilly, Walt's girlfriend—and wife-to-be—loved the cartoons, but not the name. "How about Mickey?" she suggested.

Walt Disney's first cartoon, released in 1928, was called *Steamboat Willie*—starring Mickey Mouse. Originally it was made as a silent film, but before it was released, it was changed to a "talkie," with Disney himself doing most of the voices. In 1932, he created *Flowers and Trees*, the first cartoon in full color. Five years later, in 1937, he made the first full-length cartoon film, *Snow White and the Seven Dwarfs*.

Today, Disney is the biggest name in animated films, and one of the biggest in entertainment in general. More than a *billion* people have seen his films and visited his theme parks, Walt Disney World and Disneyland.

Armor

2

The earliest type of body armor was a shirt layered with rib bones, strips of hardened leather, or slats of hardwood. The Vikings, Asians, and some Native Americans wore armor of this type. Interestingly, and to the surprise of white explorers, the men of a number of Native American tribes wore copper armor. In the Southwest (especially in what are now the states of Arizona, Colorado, and New Mexico), warriors went into battle with copper shields, breastplates, and wrist guards.

In 1933, a man wearing a medieval suit of armor tried to burglarize a house in Paris. Spotting the clanking heap of metal, the owner pushed the fool down some stairs, piled furniture on top of him, and then called the police.

The Greeks made their armor of bronze, an alloy of copper and tin. To protect their upper bodies, soldiers wore large bronze plates, with the chest and back plates joined by leather suspenders over the shoulders. They also wore ornate bronze helmets, many designed in such a way as to almost completely encase the head. There were openings for the eyes and mouth, and broad metal wings to protect the cheeks and nose. Felt or leather was used as a lining.

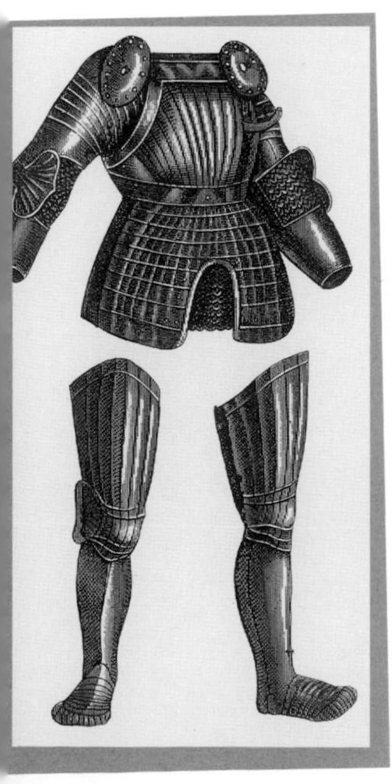

Around 400 B.C., the Romans created the first-known chain-mail armor, which con-

Knights in full battle armor

The first real test of a Kevlar vest occurred just before Christmas in 1975 in Seattle, Washington. Police officer Ray Johnson, off-duty but in uniform, was standing in a checkout line at a supermarket when suddenly a gun-wielding man tried to rob the store. Seeing Johnson, the robber shot him twice, and from only three feet away. Johnson happened to be wearing a Kevlar vest; the bullets knocked the wind out of him and bruised his chest—but that's all.

So far, Kevlar vests have saved the lives of more than 1,300 law-enforcement officers.

sisted of tiny interlocking metal rings. Out of the chain mail, they made protective shirts and skirts. They also made "scale armor"—shirts, pants, and even body suits completely covered with small, overlapping metal disks.

During the Middle Ages (A.D. 400-1450), armor became increasingly elaborate and heavy. European knights wore hoods of mail, which covered the head and neck, and long metal coats of mail that hung from the shoulders to the knees. These coats were so heavy that it took two men just to carry one! Because of the great weight, a knight could hardly move around on his own, and he had to be mounted on a horse in order to be able to fight.

Mail had another disadvantage: it did not provide a rigid, glancing surface to deflect arrows, spears, and lances. Consequently, during the thirteenth and fourteenth centuries, steel-plate body suits gradually replaced those of chain mail. Great skill was required to design and construct them. Not only did they need to offer as much protection as possible, but it was of equal importance that they bend properly at the joints. Usually this was achieved by means of creating overlapping metal parts held together (on the inside) by leather straps.

Body armor became useless following the introduction of gunpowder and firearms in Europe in the late fourteenth and early fifteenth centuries. Bullets could easily pierce most armor plate; by the end of the seventeenth century, almost all European armies had abandoned suits of armor.

Not until World War I did armor begin to make a comeback. Machine gunners and snipers wore steel backplates and breastplates in addition to helmets. Tank crews were issued metal faceplates, from which hung short curtains of mail to protect the mouth and chin.

During World War II (1939–1945) and the Vietnam War (in the 1960s and early '70s), soldiers wore flak jackets made of nylon and metal. Extremely heavy and not always effective, they were replaced in 1975 by a different type of bulletproof vest. It contained no metal, only Kevlar, a lightweight but super-strong synthetic material invented by Stephanie Kwolek, a chemist at the DuPont Company.

In the near future, soldiers may make a complete return to full body armor—of the space-age variety. This modern-day battle suit (currently being tested by the U.S. military) is made of flexible plastic; it is inflammable, impervious to chemicals, and bulletproof. The head-encompassing helmet has a voice- and data-communications unit; its eyepiece contains binocular and night-vision systems, and at any time a digitized battlefield map can be summoned and displayed right before the wearer's eyes. Instead of a rifle, the soldier carries a computerized device that doubles as a camera and powerful weapon that fires laser-guided particle beams.

The first guns were extremely small, handheld cannons. Some weighed only a pound or two, were very small, and could be fired by one person. Others were quite large and heavy (up to 20 pounds), and it took at least two people to fire it; one soldier held and aimed the weapon while the other fired.

People were not the only ones to wear armor. Horses and attack dogs were sometimes fitted with it, too!

Artificial Eyes

Corpses don't need eyes.

That's what makes it all the creepier, all the more strange. You see, the first artificial eyes were for the dead!

As far back as the ninth century B.C., the Egyptians mummified the dead, especially their kings and queens. First, the bodily organs were removed and the body cavity stuffed with cloth, sawdust, and spices. Next, the brain was extracted, piece by piece, through the nose, after which the skull was filled with a tarlike substance. Then it was time for the eyes....

The most unusual recipient of a glass eye was a snake at the London Zoo. The eye was implanted for purely medical—not cosmetic—reasons.

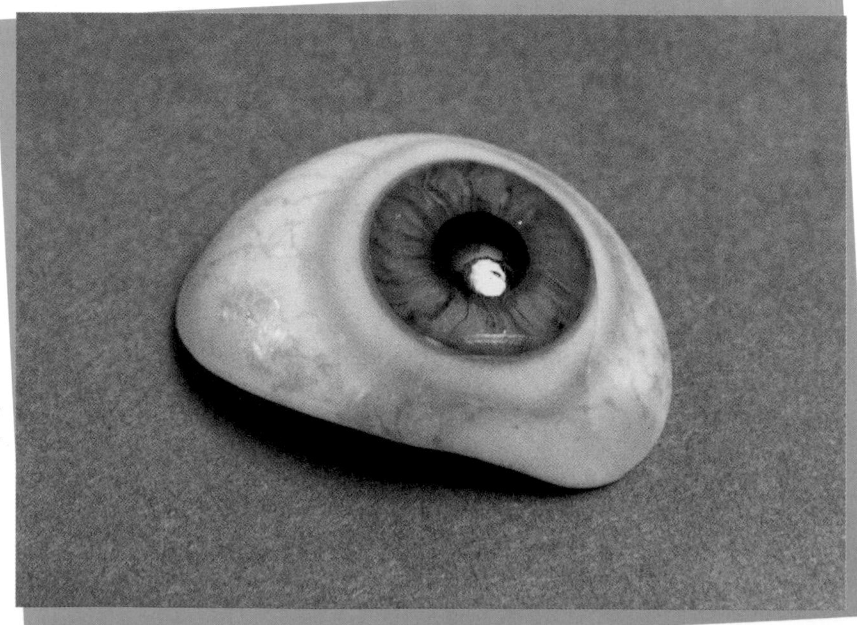

Glass eye from the early twentieth century

Etching of a man of the nineteeth century wearing an eye patch

After they were removed, plaster or wax was poured into the empty sockets. Before it hardened, precious gems were inserted. Sometimes two large rubies were used; more often, it was two emeralds or two rounded, polished pieces of jade. Often, the eyes—the precious gems—were stolen by grave robbers.

True prosthetic eyes, those for living people, were devised by Roman priest-physicians in the fifth century B.C. They were highly polished balls of stone or wood, the iris and pupil hand-painted by artists.

Glass eyes came into being in Venice in 1579. Some were solid glass; others were in the form of oval shells. Both kinds were usually ill-fitting and extremely uncomfortable to wear. The eye also tended to "roam": if it drifted toward the nose, it made the person look cross-eyed; if it drifted outward, it gave the person a "walleyed" look; and sometimes it revolved completely inside out and left only the back of the eye showing.

Today most artificial eyes are made of lightweight plastic; many are connected to muscles in the socket so that they move normally.

Before the invention of artificial eyes, it was common to sew the eyelid shut. An eye patch covered the area. For most, this was a hardened and shaped piece of leather or heavy cloth; for royalty, there were ornate patches of intricate beadwork, even of gold and gems!

During a dinner in Venice, Italy, in 1582, a man started to choke on his food. Other diners tried to help by pounding him on the back. The force of their blows knocked his artificial eye from his head, and it plopped into the soup of the woman sitting next to him.

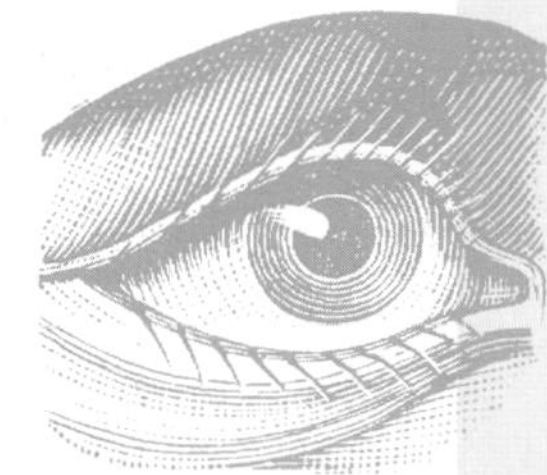

4

Baby Bottle

It sounds too silly to be true. But the first-known baby bottle was a dried cow's udder! In Europe, people removed the udder from a dead cow and dried it in the sun. Then it was filled with milk and used to feed infants!

During the eighteenth century, 75 percent of children died before the age of two. Unsanitary baby bottles were one of the primary causes.

By the twelfth century, the udders had been tossed. A less crude item came into use—an earthenware jug with two open-

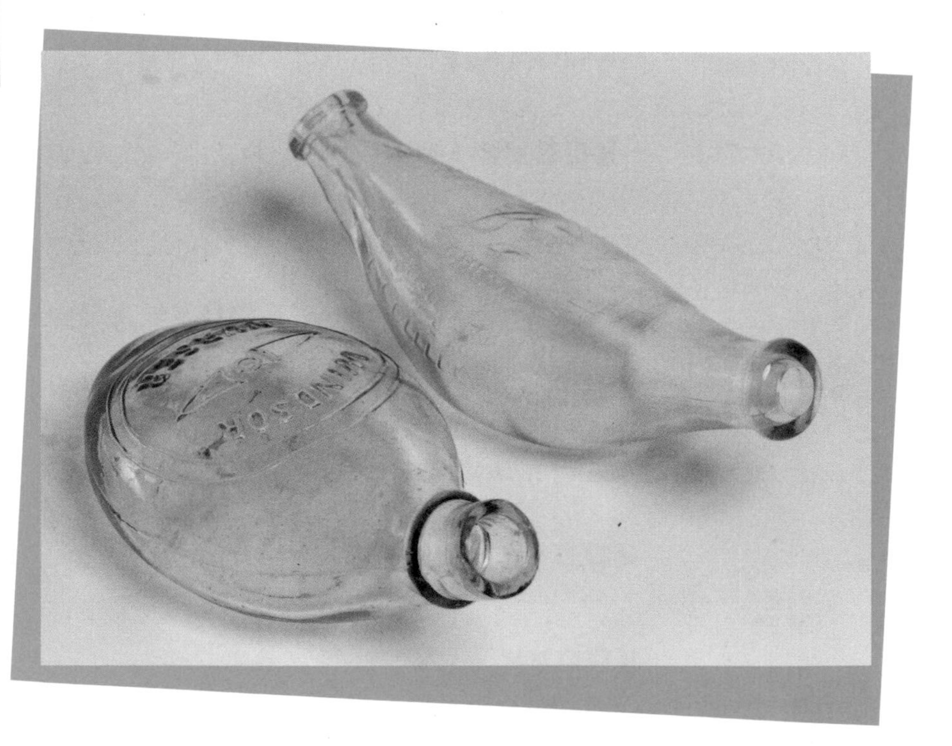

Left: *The flask-shaped glass baby bottle was patented in 1891.* **Right:** *The banana-shaped baby bottle, open at both ends, was patented four years later, in 1895.*

Even after they came to be widely known as "murder bottles," long-tube feeders remained popular. They were still being offered for sale in the Sears, Roebuck catalog of 1908.

ings. One opening was for pouring milk into the bottle, and the other, with a nipplelike attachment, was put into the baby's mouth. Some of these jugs had animal shapes; for example, a sixteenth-century bottle from England was made in the form of a duck, with the infant being fed from the bill.

The first glass baby bottle was patented in the U.S. in 1841. It was shaped like a female breast and was put over the mother's own breast to create "a useful deception."

Glass baby bottles of various shapes and designs began to appear in the seventeenth century. Most had a nipple attached directly to the narrow neck of the bottle. In the eighteenth century, the "sucking bottle" was developed. At first, instead of glass, these bottles were made of pewter, silver, or china.

Later came the "long-tube feeder." Invented in England in 1860, the device consisted of a glass bottle with a long rubber tube. On one end of the tube was a nipple; the other end extended down to the bottom of the bottle.

In 1903, Michael Owens invented the automatic bottle-making machine. The device could produce more than fourteen *thousand* bottles a day instead of the two hundred that a skilled glassblower could produce.

Because thousands of infants using them died, this type of feeder came to be known as the "murder bottle." The reason: the interior of the lengthy tube was extremely hard to clean; it thus became a breeding ground for deadly bacteria.

The rubber-tube nursing bottle was not the only dangerous type. Many early bottles had narrow necks, were flat in shape, or had some other design feature that made them very difficult to wash out.

In 1894, the infant daughter of Dr. William Decker, a New York physician, became very sick with an intestinal illness. Suspecting the cause to be contaminated bottles, Dr. Decker invented the Hygeia, a cylindrical bottle with a wide neck and a large rubber nipple. The new bottle was so successful that Dr. Decker left his practice in 1901 to run his Hygeia Nursing Bottle Company.

By the mid-twentieth century, glass was replaced with plastic, which is both lighter and safer. Today most such bottles use disposable soft-plastic liners, which eliminate the need for sterilization.

The TempGuard, a brand of baby bottle patented in the U.S. in 1944, came equipped with a thermometer attached to the side to indicate the temperature of the milk. Unfortunately, because heat-resistant glue had not yet been invented, the thermometer fell off after the bottle was boiled a few times.

Nipples have been changing right along with the bottles. The first were drilled wooden pegs, the tips of cow's horns, or small, rounded plugs of leather. Next came nipples made from rolled-up pieces of cloth, with one end inserted into the liquid-filled container and the other into the baby's mouth. Sometimes a tubelike length of sponge was used instead.

Rubber nipples appeared on the market in the nineteenth century and quickly replaced those made of other materials. In some cases the rubber was used to cushion a metal nipple, which was attached to a spring mechanism that increased the flow of liquid. Most modern nipples are made of synthetic rubber or soft silicone plastic.

Silver nipples like this one were attached to corks that fit into the open end of glass baby bottles.

Birthday Cake

Until relatively recent times, people hardly ever observed birthdays. As for children, their birthdays were *never* celebrated!

In 3000 B.C., the Egyptians started the idea of birthday parties, but these were only for the birthdays of kings and queens. Basically, the parties were lavish feasts. The *guests* all got presents, but not the person whose birthday it was.

For a brief period, the Greeks picked up the custom of celebrating birthdays—but only those of noblemen or of gods and goddesses. An important part of the festivities was a large, sweet birthday cake—which, as today, was cut up and served to guests. For the birthday of Artemis, the Greek goddess of the moon, the cake was topped with large, lighted candles.

The early Christians did not believe in birthday celebrations of any kind. Instead, they celebrated *death* days! To them, the day a person died—and went to heaven—was the important event. Most incredible of all, the early Christians did not even celebrate Christ's birth. Not until the fourth century was it finally decided by the Catholic Church that there should be a "Christmas," a mass (religious service) to honor Christ's birth.

Around the same time that Christmas came into being, so

Slaves, servants, and commoners were all invited to Egyptian birthday feasts. And this was often a day when prisoners were released from jail.

Contrary to popular belief, it is the death days and not the birthdays of Christian saints that are celebrated and have become their "feast days."

A fancy birthday party in New York City, 1897

The last *Kinderfeste* celebrated by a child was his twelfth. At thirteen, the child was considered an adult.

"Happy Birthday to You," now sung when the birthday cake arrives, was originally entitled "Good Morning to All." The song was written by two Kentucky sisters, and the music and lyrics for "Good Morning" were first published in an 1893 book, *Song Stories for Children.* The words "Happy Birthday to You" were added later.

did the birthday party as we know it. But then it was only for children. The custom began in Germany and was called a *Kinderfeste*—literally, "children's party."

A *Kinderfeste* started just before dawn. The birthday child was awakened by his or her whole family and by the arrival of a cake surrounded by lighted candles. The number of candles was always one more than the child's age, the extra one symbolizing "the light of life." As they burned down, the candles were changed and kept lit throughout the entire day, until after dinner, when the cake was eaten for dessert. Then, as now, the child blew out the candles after making a wish.

The cake was always the most important part of the *Kinderfeste*, but the birthday child also received gifts. According to German lore, the gifts were brought while the child was sleeping by the "Birthday Man," a bearded, always smiling, oversize elf. Not until the birthday cake was eaten could the presents from the Birthday Man be opened.

Blood Transfusion

6

It's a ghoulish story. A scary one.

The first recorded attempt to transfer blood from one human being to another took place in 1492. While Columbus was on his way to the New World, Pope Innocent VIII lay dying in Rome. His personal physician had given up all hope, but a foreign surgeon suggested that "an infusion of young blood" might rejuvenate the Holy Father. Blood from three young boys was injected into his veins. The pope died. So did the boys, who had literally been bled to death. The imaginative but unsuccessful surgeon fled.

The second attempt at blood transfusion is another creepy story....

The body of an adult male contains about five liters of blood (a little over a gallon), which travels through 60,000 miles of blood vessels. Placed end to end, they would stretch more than two times around the world!

Romans rushed into the gladiatorial arena to drink the blood of dying victims as a method of rejuvenating themselves.

Engraving of a seventeenth-century transfusion of blood from a lamb to a man. At the left, the man's blood is being released to make room for the incoming flow from the lamb. (Not until the nineteenth century was it discovered that blood vessels automatically adjust to increased supply.)

More than a century and a half later, in 1667, a teenage French boy lay dying. He had come down with a fever. The first doctor that his mother had summoned had "bled" the boy. One of the most common (and idiotic) medical procedures of the time, bleeding was a technique in which blood was drained from a person in the belief that this removed impurities from the body.

During the American Civil War (1861–1865) blood typing had not yet been discovered, and blood transfusion was tried only twice. One patient died; the other lived.

Seeing that he was only getting worse, the boy's mother sent for a new doctor, Dr. J. Denys, who told her that her son was dying—not from fever but from blood loss. He had lost almost a quart! Dr. Denys, using an experimental procedure, gave the boy nine ounces of sheep's blood. Amazingly, he recovered fully.

American scientists have developed an artificial blood called Oxygent. The milky substitute is most frequently used when a patient refuses transfusions of real blood on religious grounds.

Dr. Denys didn't know it, but he had just been lucky. Usually, animal blood and human blood don't mix.

In the coming months, Denys used the procedure several more times. His results were increasingly poor. Then the inevitable happened: one of his patients died—in great agony. The practice was discontinued.

Not until 1818, over 150 years later, was transfusion tried again. Though human blood was used, the patient became extremely ill.

In 1900 came the real breakthrough, the discovery of different blood types and how to identify them. Finally, transfusion had become the reliable, sane, lifesaving procedure doctors had long hoped it would be. Since then, countless lives have been saved by receiving blood transfusions.

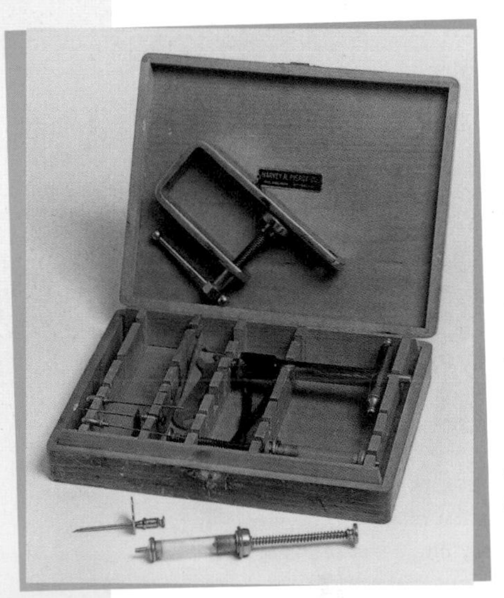

A doctor's blood transfusion kit, 1924

Books

7

If it wouldn't be too much trouble, would you mind copying this book by hand? And when you're done, please copy the Bible. It'll only take you a few years.

Incredibly, *all* books were originally made this way. Books in the form familiar to us—made of bound-together pages—came into being in the second century. Until the fifteenth century, each one of them was copied by hand by a Christian monk working in a cold, dreary monastery. Though some of the monks were highly educated, many could not even read what they were writing! All they did, year after year, was copy what was in front of them.

The Egyptians and the Romans wrote on clay tablets and, later, papyrus scrolls. The Christian monks wrote on vellum, very thin and carefully cured animal skin. Not until the fourteenth century did they use paper.

A monk learns about eyestrain and writer's cramp by copying a book by hand.

There was no punctuation or any spacing between the words in early books; everything was run together. The ancient Greeks were the first to use any punctuation: every now and then they'd toss in a vertical line to show the separation between sentences. The early Christians (second century) continued the idea. Their writings often began with a cross; a leaf or other design was sometimes placed at the ends of sentences.

The famous French author Honoré de Balzac (1799–1850) emulated the Christian monks. For the last twenty-one years of his life he wrote daily for eighteen hours, always wearing a monk's cowl and standing at his desk.

Typesetters preparing to print a book from movable type

Menelik II (1844–1913) former emperor of Ethiopia, had a weird habit. Whenever he was feeling nervous or ill, he would eat a few pages of the Bible. "It never fails to make me feel better," he proclaimed. But one day when he was feeling especially bad, he ordered a servant to tear the entire Book of Kings from an Egyptian edition of the Bible. Menelik ate every page of it—and died, apparently from partaking of too much of a good thing.

It took Margaret Mitchell ten years to write *Gone with the Wind.*

Four new books are published in the United States every hour.

Producing books in great quantities was not possible until the invention of printing from movable type—arranging individual letters in a frame to form the words on a page. Though the first such book was the *Diamond of Sutra*, published in Korea in 1409, modern printing did not really get going until 1456, when Johann Gutenberg of Germany printed full-length editions of the Bible. Interestingly, not only was the Bible the first major work ever printed; it is now, and has been for centuries, the number-one best-selling book in the world.

The first paperback books were published in 1841. Though printed in Germany, the books were in English and were intended for sale to British and American tourists. Oddly, upon buying a paperback, the purchaser had to agree to throw it away when finished! If a bookseller did that today, you'd think he was either joking or totally nuts.

Camera

8

It took eight hours to "snap" the first photograph.

In the summer of 1826, Frenchman Joseph Niepce mounted a wooden camera on the windowsill of an upstairs room and then took a picture of the view behind his house. It shows a pigeon-house on the left, a pear tree, and a barn. The picture was captured not on film but on a light-sensitive piece of metal. The shutter of the camera had to be kept open for over *eight hours* before the image appeared.

By 1839, Louis Daguerre, another Frenchman, had reduced the exposure time to between fifteen and thirty minutes. One of his earliest pictures is of a boulevard in Paris. Though it was full of people, the boulevard appears spookily empty. Why?

Niepce's very first photograph was lost in 1898 and not recovered until 1952, when it turned up in an attic in England.

George Eastman made up the word *Kodak*. *K* was his favorite letter because it was the first letter of his mother's name. Thus he decided to give the camera—and film—a name that began and ended with *K*. Fiddling with different letter combinations, he came up with *Kodak*.

Built for the 1900 Paris Exposition, the Mammoth camera took mammoth photos! The pictures were 4 1/2 by 8 feet. The camera weighed 1,400 pounds and a crew of fifteen was needed to operate it.

The Kodak Brownie camera originally cost one dollar. Eastman named it the "Brownie" because he loved the children's books of Canadian author Palmer Cox, whose colorful works were populated by happy, efficient elves called brownies.

Eastman hated to have his picture taken; very few photos of him exist.

Because the process was still so slow that only stationary objects could be captured on camera.

In 1888, George Eastman, an American, introduced the Kodak box camera. The Kodak was the first camera designed specifically for mass production and amateur use. It was lightweight, inexpensive, and easy to operate.

The Kodak system also eliminated the need for photographers to process their own pictures. The camera used a roll of gelatin-coated film that could take one hundred round photographs. After a roll had been used, the photographer sent the camera with the film inside to one of Eastman's processing plants. The plant developed the film, made prints, and then returned the camera loaded with a new roll of film. The Kodak slogan declared: "You Press the Button. We Do the Rest."

The Folding Brownie, 1905

The Brownie 127, 1952

The Advantix Fun Saver, 1998

The evolution of the snapshot camera

Circus

9

The Romans invented the circus. The word itself is Latin, and means "circle" or "ring."

Every Roman circus started with a parade—a noisy, crazy one. There were musicians, people carrying statues of gods, and chariots pulled by everything from lions to giraffes. The parade would wind its way through the city; then everyone would go to an open-air arena. Admission was free; however, as now, vendors worked the stands, selling food and drinks.

The first event was usually the chariot race. Just about anything and everything was legal. The charioteers would hack and jab at each other with swords and spears. The wheels sometimes had "hubcaps" consisting of vicious, rapidly rotating knives.

Other parts of the circus were even more frightening and bloody. Fights were to the death. Boxers wore spiked gloves. Gladiators armed with swords, axes, and knives battled each other—or fought for their lives against wild animals. In a single circus, it was recorded that 11,000 animals were killed.

The Roman emperor Commodus especially favored fights between men and animals. Often he sat in the stands with a bow and arrow in hand. He would wait until an animal was about to kill a man, then he'd shoot the animal.

The Circus Maximus, the largest in Rome, had roughly 150,000 seats. Two thousand gladiators died in a circus celebrating Rome's one thousandth anniversary.

One day in England, in 1769, Major Philip Astley found a diamond ring on a bridge, sold it at a good price, and used the money to start the first circus of modern times. The show consisted mostly of equestrian (horse) acts.

This engraving, showing many acts in one ring, was originally used to advertise a nineteenth-century circus.

Rickett's Circus was the first in the United States. It opened in Philadelphia in 1792. In 1793, one of the spectators at Rickett's Circus was President George Washington.

The first known use of elephants in a modern circus occurred in France in 1816. Among other tricks, the elephant used its trunk to uncork a bottle of water and then drink it.

Julius Caesar liked a different sort of fight. Once he had the entire arena floor flooded and turned into a lake! Ships were brought in, and the men on them fought a "sea battle."

Sideshows also had their start in Rome. People who were deformed or different in some way were put in cages for others to see and make fun of.

Clowns in the Roman circus, like the clowns of today, wore goofy clothes and loads of makeup. They engaged in all sorts of antics, including making jokes about the people in the stands and throwing things at them. The clowns were there mostly for comic relief, but even *their* lives were sometimes in danger. In one act, two clowns ran and got into baskets at either end of a seesaw; then a lion was set free in the ring. When it came after one of the clowns, he would push off—and up—into the air. Then, as the animal charged toward the basket on the ground, that clown would suddenly go up and out of reach. The spectators thought this was great for a laugh, especially if one of the clowns didn't push off in time and got torn to pieces by the lion.

Today, of course, the circus is very different. The Roman emperors are gone. People no longer fight to the death. Animals are not killed for sport. And clowns do not play deadly, bloody games. But when circuses began, that's how it was.

Clothes Washer and Dryer

10

Early electric washing machines were manually filled with buckets of water and were also drained by hand. The wash "cycle" continued until the operator decided to pull the plug.

Question: How did the Pilgrims wash their clothes during their voyage to America? Answer: The same way it had been done at sea for centuries. They placed their dirty laundry in a strong cloth bag, tossed it overboard, and dragged it behind the ship for hours. It worked pretty well, and did what washing machines today do: it forced water through the clothes while tumbling and turning them every which way.

During the 1800s, all sorts of hand-operated washers were invented. The first was a wooden barrel and a device called a dolly, a big plunger that was pushed up and down by hand. Next, around 1860, came "the box." Soap, water, and laundry were put into a sealed wooden box held between two support beams and turned around and around by means of a hand crank. In 1884 a man named Morton invented one of the best of the hand-operated devices. "It is so easy to work," Morton boasted in an early advertisement, "that a child can wash six sheets in fifteen minutes!"

From 1912 to 1918, the U.S. Treasury Department actually washed, dried, and ironed dirty money! Operated by two people, the machine could clean as many as forty thousand notes a day. The dirty bills were placed between long, moving belts, then bathed in a mixture of soap, water, and germicide. Finally, the bills were dried and ironed.

In 1914, electric motors were introduced, finally putting all the hand cranking to an end. At first, these motors were fitted right under the tub, with their inner workings exposed. Water from the washer dribbled down into them, frequently giving

Commercial laundering in the United States owes its start to the California gold rush of 1849. A miner named Davis failed to find gold, so he started a laundry near Oakland, California. At first he washed clothes in a barrel. Then Charles Mattee designed a crude wooden wash wheel for him, and other improvements followed.

A washer made by a Swedish company called Asko uses less than *six* gallons of water in a complete cycle, as compared with forty-eight to fifty gallons in a regular washing machine! It uses fast "tumbling action" to force the water and soap through the clothes. This washer also saves electricity: it spins clothes until most of the water is gone, so very little time in the dryer is needed.

the operator a paralyzing shock. "My hair stood on end and me eyeballs almost shot right out of me head," a woman of the era wrote in her diary.

In the 1920s, mechanical tubs were introduced, and the washing machine as we know it had finally come to be. To prevent shocks, the motor was kept apart from the tub and was fully enclosed.

The first dryer was a fairly worthless contraption. Called the "Ventilator," it was invented in 1800 by M. Pochon of France. Damp, hand-wrung clothes were dumped into a cylindrical metal drum pierced with holes, and as a handle was turned, the drum rotated above an open fire. Depending on the size of the fire, the clothes either took forever to dry or burned, and they always stank of soot and smoke.

J. R. Moore invented the first successful electric dryer in the 1930s. Moore sold his invention to the Hamilton Company in Wisconsin, who called in industrial designer Brooks Stevens to help redesign the machine. Stevens came up with the idea for a window in the dryer's door so that consumers would know what the machine was for. He advised the company to display the window-type dryer in stores with a "pair of boxer shorts flying around in there."

Despite the fact that the dryers worked, and despite the flying shorts, sales were poor. Not until the early 1960s did they really catch on, and people began abandoning their clotheslines in favor of mechanical dryers.

Contact Lenses

The first man to wear contact lenses had good eyesight. No problem there. But he did have another problem, and a pretty nasty one. He had a disease of the inside of the eyelid.

The year: 1887. The place: Switzerland. Dr. A. E. Fick was treating the man for his eye condition, and Dr. Fick was worried. The various medications he was using to try to clear up his patient's disease were not working very well, and he was afraid

In his work to perfect contact lenses, Dr. Fick tried them on rabbits, cadavers, and then his own eyes.

In 1930, nearsighted model Grace Robins put on the first public demonstration of how to insert and wear contacts.

Soft contact lenses, invented by Bausch & Lomb, first became available in 1960.

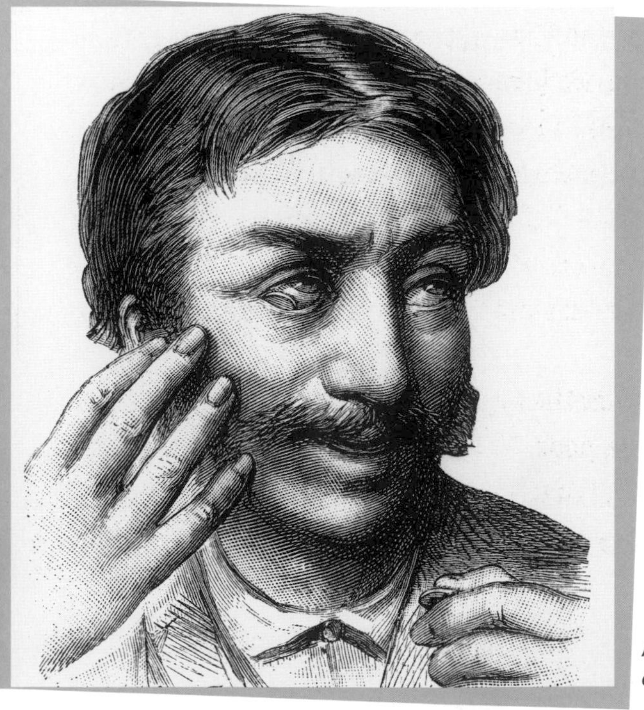

A man inserting a glass contact lens. Ouch!

it was going to spread to the man's eyes and destroy his sight.

Suddenly, during one of the man's visits to his clinic, Dr. Fick had an idea. He made careful measurements of his patient's eyes and, after applying ointment to the inside of his lids, told him to come back in a couple of days.

When the man returned, Dr. Fick had a pair of small, odd-looking glass cups. "I had a glassblower make these," he said. "For now, I'm calling them 'eye-contact lenses.' "

The man was a bit leery of the strange-looking things. But to save his sight, he was willing to try anything.

Dr. Fick had him lie back on a surgical table. Then, with the assistance of a nurse, he placed the contact lenses on the man's eyes. The bowl-shaped glass lenses covered almost the entire eyeball, not just the cornea. The things were kind of goofy-looking, and they were thick and uncomfortable to wear, but they saved the man's sight.

Soon Dr. Fick was making more contact lenses. These were smaller, made of thinner glass, and far more comfortable. And they had a whole different purpose than the first lenses. They were designed to improve vision—and they did.

Today contact lenses are made of plastic, either hard or soft. In the United States alone, more than 38 million people wear them.

Contact lenses are still used to help people with eye deformities and diseases. For example, keratoconus is a condition in which the eye bulges out at its center, creating blurred images that ordinary glasses cannot correct.

Contacts are not the newest means of correcting vision. Doctors today are able to perform laser surgery to correct numerous vision problems. In some instances, people who have worn glasses or contacts their entire lives can have their problem corrected by surgical procedures lasting only ten to fifteen minutes!

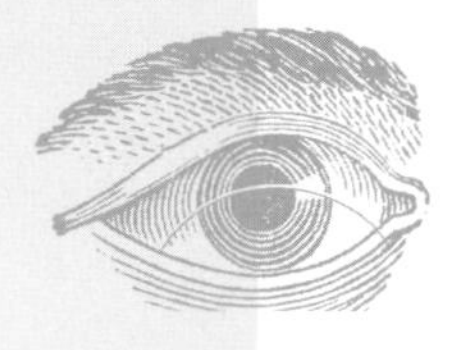

Deodorant

Napoleon stank. He smelled so bad that people around him could hardly stand it. He rarely bathed. Instead, he drenched himself in cologne almost every day. That was the famous Frenchman's deodorant.

On a hot day (in a twenty-four-hour period), a human adult can sweat as much as three gallons.

Actually, for a long time in Europe, Napoleon's dumb concept of a deodorant was all that was around. People either did nothing about their body odor or they put on some kind of perfume—and smelled even worse, only sweeter and weirder.

The Egyptians, three thousand years earlier, smelled a lot better than Napoleon. They bathed, preferably in water that had been lightly scented. Then they did one of the most important things to prevent underarm odor: they shaved their armpits.

Both men and women did it—partly because they thought underarm hair was ugly, partly because they had discovered that shaving it off helped stop body odor in its tracks. The reason why shaving helps (as scientists would figure out centuries later) is that hair is a perfect place for bacteria to grow. When alive, the bacteria are odorless; but then they die and decompose, which is when they (and underarms) start smelling gross.

In old age, the apocrine sweat glands in the underarms sometimes become almost completely inactive.

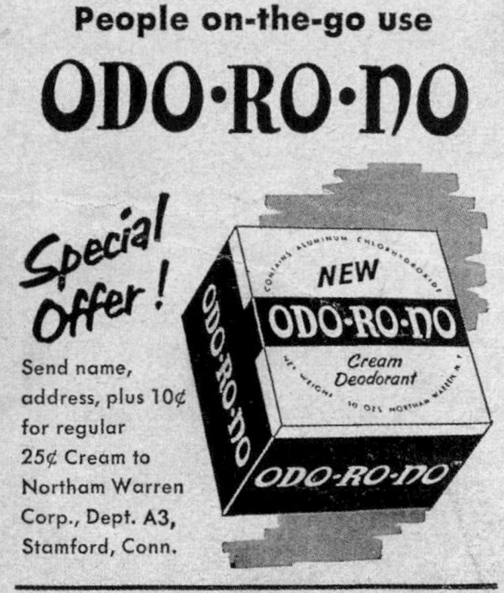

An ad for Odo-Ro-No deodorant, 1953

After bathing and shaving their ancient underarms, the ancient Egyptians then applied homemade deodorants. Some used perfumed oils. Others splashed on lemon juice or a concoction made of ground-up cinnamon and water.

Such deodorants covered up odor but did not get to the source of another problem: underarm wetness.

In the nineteenth century, scientists in the United States discovered sweat glands—and that we have two kinds in our skin: eccrine and apocrine. Eccrine glands constantly clean pores and regulate body temperature. You have over 2 million of them in your skin, and although they are distributed over your entire body, they are much more dense in some areas than others. For example, the palms of your hands have approximately 2,500 per square inch; the backs of your hands have fewer than 500 for the same area.

The apocrine sweat glands are the ones that cause body odor; they're also really peculiar. They completely cover the body's surface at birth (which gives babies their special aroma). But then, as the child grows, these glands shrivel up! Scientists do not know why, but the apocrine glands all disappear—except for those in the armpit area. During childhood, they are almost totally inactive. Then comes puberty, when hormones switch on these glands. That's when you have to start trotting off to the drugstore to get deodorants and antiperspirants.

As pit sniffers can attest, it's the pits that make the biggest stink. At Hill Top Research, Inc., of Cincinnati, Ohio, the effectiveness of underarm deodorants is tested. First, odor judges get a good whiff of the unfumigated underarms of paid volunteers. After the application of deodorants to the test group's armpits, the judges all start nosing around again. How would you like to have *that* job?

Antiperspirants are chemicals used to stop the underarm apocrine glands from producing moisture. Deprived of moisture, bacteria simply cannot multiply.

The first antiperspirant was Mum, which was introduced in the U.S. in 1888. It came in a jar and consisted of zinc, a drying chemical, in a cream base. Everdry hit the market in 1902, followed in 1908 by Hush and in 1914 by Odo-Ro-No. These were the first antiperspirants to use another drying compound, aluminum chloride, which is found in most modern products.

During these early days, only women used antiperspirants—probably because all the ads were directed at females. Not until the 1930s did companies begin to target the male market. It took them long enough, but they finally realized that men don't want to be smelly and sweaty, either!

Disposable Diaper

The Procter & Gamble Company spent more research money on disposable diapers than Henry Ford spent on his first automobile.

Kenneth Buell, a man known for his work on the Gemini space program, designed Luvs, another diaper brand produced by Procter & Gamble.

For many centuries in Europe, a newborn baby was always wrapped up in heavy swaddling bandages until it was unable to make even the slightest movement. Such swaddling, said physicians of the time, kept "bad air out and the nourishing juices in." Diapers were usually changed *only once a day*. (Yuck!) Doing so more often was considered hazardous to the baby's health!

By the twentieth century, this strange, stinky way of taking care of babies had long been dumped. Off went the swaddling and on went the diapers—several times a day. That pretty much solved the babies' problem, but not that of the parents. They were stuck with the never-ending chore of washing, bleaching, and drying "nappies," as they were then called.

Naturally, it was the mother of a newborn who figured out how to deal with diapers faster and more easily. Her name was Marion Donovan. One day in 1950, she took a piece of shower curtain, cut it down to size, and lined it with inexpensive padding. In that moment, she created the world's first disposable diaper. She called it the "Boater," because, like a good boat, it was watertight.

Donovan expected manufacturers to be as excited about her

invention as she was. They weren't. So she began marketing Boaters herself. Within a few years, she had made a small fortune, but her invention *really* paid off when she sold the patent to the Procter & Gamble Company for over a million dollars.

On April 21, 1959, Bertha A. Dlugi filed for a patent on diapers for birds. So far, neither birds nor manufacturers have shown any interest in the idea.

The first "throwaway" mass-produced diapers made by Procter & Gamble had elasticized waistbands and leg openings. But new parents weren't buying: the things fit poorly, were uncomfortable, and usually leaked. In 1961 the company introduced Pampers, the basic design of which is still the standard today—a rayon-plastic outer garment with a highly absorbent lining.

A patent lasts for only seventeen years, and now there are many competitive brands on the market. But since 1961 there have been only two important changes in the product. First, adhesive tabs were added (to replace potentially dangerous safety pins). More recently, manufacturers began coming out with models designed differently for girls and boys.

By the 1980s, most babies in the United States wore disposable diapers. But now the trend is beginning to reverse, and many people are going back to the washable variety. The reason: concern about the environment and about the millions of plastic diapers going into landfills each year.

An ad from the 1950s for Chux, an early brand of disposable diapers

14 Eraser

One day in 1564 in Europe, a storm knocked over a huge tree. In the ground from which it had been uprooted was a hard, blackish substance, which eventually came to be known as graphite. From graphite, the first pencils were made.

Naturally, as soon as people started using pencils, they started making mistakes. And to get rid of their blunders and goof-ups, they needed erasers—the first of which, as it turned

Rubber gets its name from the fact that its first use was as an eraser. Pencil marks could be erased by "rubbing" them with the material.

In nineteenth-century England, pencil makers used yellow paint to cover the imperfect wood used in their pencils. To this day, yellow is the most common color for pencils.

out, were edible! Believe it or not, the first erasers were pieces of bread.

Though not very effective, bread lasted for almost two centuries as the world's only type of eraser. Not until 1752 did the rubber eraser come into being, the invention of a Frenchman by the name of Magellan.

With the invention of word-processing systems, a new type of eraser came into being: by tapping a key or two, a word, page, or even an entire document can be erased.

About twenty years later, erasers reached England. There the first mention of them appears in 1770 in a book by Joseph Priestley, who wrote: "I have seen a substance excellently adapted to the purpose of wiping from a paper the marks of a black-lead pencil. It is sold by Mr. Nairne, [who] sells a cubical piece of about half an inch for three shillings [fifteen cents], and he says it will last for several years."

Many years later, in 1858, an American inventor named Hyman Lipman really topped things off. It was Lipman who came up with the idea of putting the eraser where it really belongs—on the end of a pencil!

False Teeth

Gross but true: the first dentures were made with teeth *from the dead*. The Etruscans, an ancient people of Italy, were wearing such teeth as early as 700 B.C. The teeth were pried from the jaws of corpses and held together in the wearer's mouth with bands of gold.

Queen Elizabeth I of England (1533–1603), disturbed by the fact that her face had sunk inward from the loss of teeth, appeared in public with her mouth stuffed with fine cloth.

In A.D. 1500, the Japanese came out with their own version. First, a wooden base was custom-made to fit snugly over the wearer's gums. Then, implanted into notches in the base were fake teeth made from bits of carved bone, marble, or ivory. Or (like the Etruscans) real teeth taken from the dead were used.

For the next three hundred years, there were no real attempts to create new types of false teeth. Then, toward the end of the seventeenth century, dentists suddenly started testing out just about every material and design imaginable. First they tried carving dentures from wood or animal bone, hingeing the upper and lower teeth with leather. Later came teeth made from walrus tusks, hippopotamus ivory, and the upper teeth from cows. (George Washington tried dentures made from all three of these materials; however, he did not, as many people believe, ever have wooden teeth.)

To disguise the hollows left by rotten teeth, well-to-do Europeans of the eighteenth century wore "plumpers," cork pads inserted between the cheek and gum.

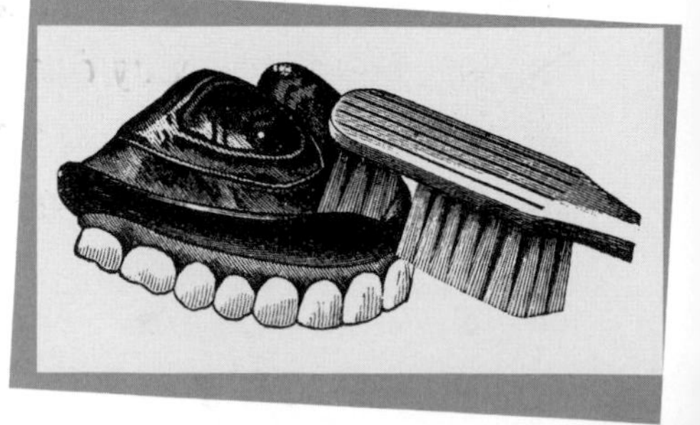

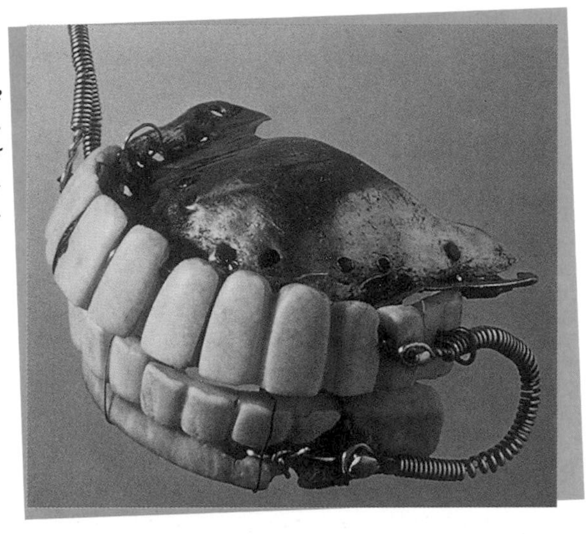

False teeth worn by George Washington in the 1790s. They were made to order for him by Dr. John Greenwood, his favorite dentist.

In England and France during the early eighteenth century, wealthy people started wearing really freaky, purely ornamental teeth. Trying to be trendy (but probably looking like complete fools), they wore teeth made of solid silver, gold, mother-of-pearl, or agate, a type of marble. Some even studded their teeth with diamonds and other precious gems.

Celluloid plastic dentures came next, in the nineteenth century. Not only did they look totally phony, they had another problem: they were highly flammable. Smokers who wore them were likely to have their teeth melt or catch on fire!

Rather than use artificial materials, some inventors in the nineteenth century made dentures out of real human teeth taken from *living* persons, not from the dead. Many Europeans during this time were so poor that, for a fee, they would have all their teeth pulled. The teeth were fashioned into a removable mounting, called a bridge, and then put into the mouth of someone who could afford them.

Keeping these early dentures in place was a big problem. Some early versions were hinged with steel springs, and the wearer would have to apply constant pressure by keeping his

When Washington first took office in 1789, he had only one of his own teeth left. The tooth soon became loose and was pulled by Washington's favorite dentist, Dr. John Greenwood. Washington gave the tooth to the dentist, who kept it on his watch chain for the rest of his life.

George Washington was buried wearing a set of false teeth made by Dr. Greenwood.

To make dentures in England during the nineteenth century, teeth taken from the dead of the American Civil War were shipped across the Atlantic by the barrelful.

Nineteenth-century denture wearers often ate at home rather than dining in public. Trying to eat with the false teeth of the time was difficult at best. And sometimes dentures were worn just for the sake of looks—they had to be taken out in order to eat!

An accident really uncanny
Befell a respectable granny;
She sat down in a chair
While her dentures
were there,
And bit herself
right in the fanny.
—Anonymous

mouth shut. An even nastier contraption required the wearer to have his gums pierced with little hooks in order to keep the dentures in place.

By the late nineteenth century, inventors had devised porcelain teeth, a big improvement over anything tried before. Then came the idea of setting the teeth into hardened rubber. After a wax impression of the wearer's mouth was made, a set of reasonably comfortable and usable dentures could be made.

Since then, dentures have continued to improve. But ironically, now that we seem to have almost perfected the art, false teeth are on the verge of becoming a thing of the past. Scientists and dentists are now directing their efforts toward the goal of growing new teeth for toothless people! Already, experiments have been done in which tiny specks of tooth from a child are transplanted into the gums of an adult. Within four to five months, new teeth begin to grow. So far, twelve people have received new teeth in this way. If such experiments continue to succeed, it is possible that in the near future the only place you will find false teeth is in a museum.

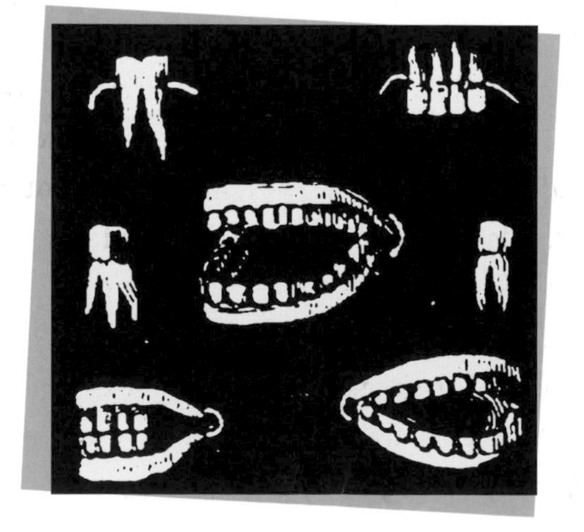

Family Names

The custom of giving last names (surnames) did not come into being until the Middle Ages. Before this time an individual had only a first name—and perhaps a title. For example: Robert, Duke of Wellington eventually changed into Robert Wellington.

The most common last name in the English-speaking world is Smith, which means "one who works with metal." Johnson is the second most common.

Some people's occupations became their last names. Catherine the Baker, for example, gradually became Catherine Baker. Many other occupations are surnames. Singer, Hunter, Miller, and Cook are just a few examples. (The same holds true for names from other languages. The name Schindler, for example, is German for a person who shingles roofs.)

Other people took on the name of a place or a local landmark. Thus a person referred to as "Albert, who lives by the rivers" would eventually become known as Albert Rivers. (Or, in Spanish, Alberto Ríos.) Desmond of York would become Desmond York. Meadows, Marsh, Field, and Lane are other names of this kind.

The first person known to have a middle name was Henry Frederick Arundel (born in 1608).

Physical characteristics and aspects of personality also turned into names. Surnames such as Moody, Brown, Strong, Wild, and Small were all derived in this way. (In Yiddish, the word for *small* is Klein—a common last name.)

Many names end in *son*. The reason is that during the Middle Ages, if your name was Brian and your father's name was John, you would have been referred to as Brian, John's son. In time, people simplified your name by calling you Brian Johnson. Just a few family names of this type include: Davidson, Robertson, Peterson, and Albertson.

Just for fun, you might want to make lists of names that fall into different categories; for example, names that are occupations, physical descriptions, or male first names plus *son*. You'll probably be surprised at how many come to mind!

One of the longest last names is that of Hawaii resident Valentine Kikahiolanikapukanehumamo-kiukakuialonoikaouiaulani. "I've spent half my life just spelling my name," he complains.

At the age of sixty-three, white-bearded Winfred Holley officially changed his name to Santa Claus. Terril Williams of Fresno, California, went for the works; he legally changed his name to God.

Two American presidents were named Johnson— Andrew Johnson and Lyndon B. Johnson.

Graham Crackers

Graham crackers started out as a health food. They were the mainstay of a health craze and religious movement, Grahamism, which swept across the United States in the 1820s and '30s.

Sylvester Graham was in chronically poor health. As a young man, he married his private nurse and later became an eccentric, self-styled minister and doctor. Obsessed with healthful eating, he traveled all over the country, preaching that the way to bodily well-being and spiritual salvation lay in a healthy diet. Drinking anything but water "ruined one's

A friend of Graham's was Dr. John Kellogg, who breakfasted daily on seven graham crackers. In addition to cornflakes, Kellogg invented granola.

In 1916, an unknown artist painted a picture of a child asleep in a high chair. Thirty years later, an artist working for Nabisco put a box of graham crackers under the child's arm—and created this advertisement.

Grahamites also believed in sleeping with the windows open, even in winter.

In Great Britain, graham crackers are called "digestive biscuits."

innards," he believed. Mustard and ketchup were also out, since they "caused insanity." Red meat was another terrible food. Eating it, claimed the minister, turned people into "perverts with bad, sexy thoughts." White bread was the worst food of all, both nutritionally and spiritually. In his opinion, it was "evil."

Graham's cure-all: substituting white bread with crackers made from unsifted whole-wheat flour. From 1830 on, Graham's followers, called Grahamites, as well as the general public, acquired a taste for his sweet, crispy creation, graham crackers.

Despite his healthy low-fat, high-fiber diet, Sylvester Graham remained a sickly man his entire life. He died at the relatively young age of fifty-seven.

The Guinness Book of Records

18

It all started because a hunter had a question he couldn't answer.

The hunter was an Englishman, Sir Hugh Beaver. One morning in 1951, he took a shot at a very fast bird called a golden plover and missed. He wondered how fast the plover had been flying and if it was the fastest bird in the world.

Sir Hugh tried to find the information in encyclopedias. None provided a definitive answer. He asked fellow hunters, but they weren't much help, either. All they did was argue!

The fruitless quarreling went on for years—not only about birds but about many subjects. Annoyed, Sir Hugh decided in 1954 that what the world needed was a book that explained what was the fastest, slowest, oldest, youngest, largest, shortest, and so forth.

But who could write such a book?

At the Guinness Brewery, where Sir Hugh was the managing director, he asked if anyone knew of a possible author. An employee at the company recommended two of his friends, identical twins Norris and Ross McWhirter. Ever since childhood, the McWhirters had shared an insatiable love of interesting facts and information. From newspapers, magazines,

As children, the McWhirter twins shared the same room—even though the house in which they lived had seven bedrooms.

Norris and Ross both graduated from Oxford, both served in the British navy, and both married and had two children.

In putting together new editions of their book, the twins claimed that they rarely needed to speak, as though communicating telepathically.

The heaviest (healthy) baby born to normal parents weighed twenty-two pounds, eight ounces! (On average, babies weigh seven pounds at birth.)

The youngest major-league baseball player was Joe Nuxhall, who started his career at the age of fifteen.

The highest tidal wave was an estimated 278 feet, which hit Ishigaki Island in the Pacific on April 24, 1971.

and reference books, the twins had made lists on subjects such as the heaviest baby, the youngest pro baseball player, and the highest tidal wave.

Sir Hugh interviewed the twins, testing their knowledge of interesting, unusual facts. He asked them question after question. The McWhirters knew all the answers, including the name of the fastest bird (the spine-tailed swift, not the golden plover). Impressed, Sir Hugh asked them if they would like to write such a book. The twins gave an enthusiastic *yes*, and started work on it immediately.

In September 1955, the first *Guinness Book of Records*, 198 pages long and bound in green leather, was in bookstores. Three months later, it was England's number-one nonfiction best-seller. Suddenly, it seemed, the whole country was enthralled with record-setting and learning interesting bits of information. By the thousands, readers wrote the McWhirters. A few questioned the accuracy of their information. Most sent facts of their own, hoping to see them included in subsequent printings.

The Guinness Book of Records offers an endless array of fascinating facts. Among these is that "the all-time copyrighted best-seller" (and for many years "the world's fastest-selling title") is, as you might have guessed, *The Guinness Book of Records*.

Hair Coloring

People have been coloring their hair for thousands of years, men more than women. Greek men bleached their hair blond—using a mixture of urine, lemon juice, and ashes. Phoenician men dusted their hair with white talc or yellow pollen. Roman men, to prevent graying, slept with a paste of crushed herbs and earthworms on their hair.

At various times in their history, Aztec men and women bleached (or streaked) their hair blond.

By the sixteenth century, especially in Europe, women started getting as silly about hair coloring as men. They dyed their hair every color imaginable. Pink, blue, yellow, green, white, and purple—each was in vogue for a time.

And then for a long time the practice of coloring hair died out almost completely. Instead, many men and women took to wearing wigs. Usually powdered white, the wigs went over the persons' real hair (or, if they didn't have any, on their bald noggins).

Gentlemen in Elizabethan England perfumed and colored their mustaches, the favorite tints being bright red, orange, and purple.

Coloring hair began to be fashionable again around 1900. In 1909, a French chemist started the first commercial hair-dye business. His name was Eugene Schueller, and at first he called his budding business the Harmless Hair Dye Company. A year later he changed this to the more glamorous-sounding L'Oréal.

Still, for the next forty years or so, most people did not color their hair. As late as 1950, only 7 percent of American women dyed their hair, and less than 1 percent of the male population.

A young woman by the name of Shirley Polykoff turned everything around. One day in 1956, Ms. Polykoff, who worked at an agency that handled advertising for Clairol came up with a catchy pair of phrases: "Does She...or Doesn't She?" and "Only Her Hairdresser Knows for Sure." Sales for Clairol—and for the whole hair-coloring industry—skyrocketed. For the first time, American women could quickly and easily color their hair at home.

Today up to 60 percent of all Americans color their hair.

Black hair was a fad among Roman men for a time. The dye was created by boiling walnut shells and leeks (a type of vegetable).

Queen Elizabeth I of England had bright, reddish orange hair. During her reign (1518–1603), both men and women dyed their hair the same color to match their queen's.

Shirley Polykoff, a "bleached blonde," thought of the Clairol slogan when her boyfriend's mother wondered whether or not she "painted her hair."

Shirley Polykoff's "Does she... or doesn't she?" ad campaign was a great success for Clairol. It also launched a hair-coloring fad in the U.S. that is still going strong today.

Ketchup

20

You're at a restaurant and want some ketchup. You tell the waiter; he brings you some. You stare at the bottle, then open it up—and decide the waiter is either a lunatic or has a really sick sense of humor. The "ketchup" he's brought you is a green-and-brown paste, and when you look at the list of ingredients, you find that the stuff is made of squished-up cucumbers, walnuts, and mushrooms. Weirdly, that's what "ketchup" was like in eighteenth-century Europe and America. But let's go back to the beginning. . . .

In 1690, the Chinese developed a thick sauce made of pickled fish and spices. They called it *ke-tsiap*, which means "tasty sauce." From China, *ke-tsiap* spread to Malaysia, where it took on the name *kechap*. Early in the eighteenth century, British sailors brought samples of the sauce back to England. Misspelling it *ketchup*, English chefs tried to duplicate it, but not knowing the original ingredients, they made a puree of salt water, cucumbers, walnuts, and mushrooms, and sometimes tossed in whatever else was handy.

In the United States, around 1790, tomatoes were added—and gradually replaced all the other ingredients. But preparation of homemade ketchup was a long, hard task. The tomatoes

It was once believed that eating tomatoes caused insanity and death. Actually, the leaves of the plant *are* poisonous; however, the tomato (which is a fruit, not a vegetable) is highly nutritious.

One of the first people in the United States to cultivate tomatoes was Thomas Jefferson.

In this 1921 ad, the company takes great pride in its "spotless Heinz kitchens." Actually, Henry Heinz was obsessed with cleanliness and healthfulness.

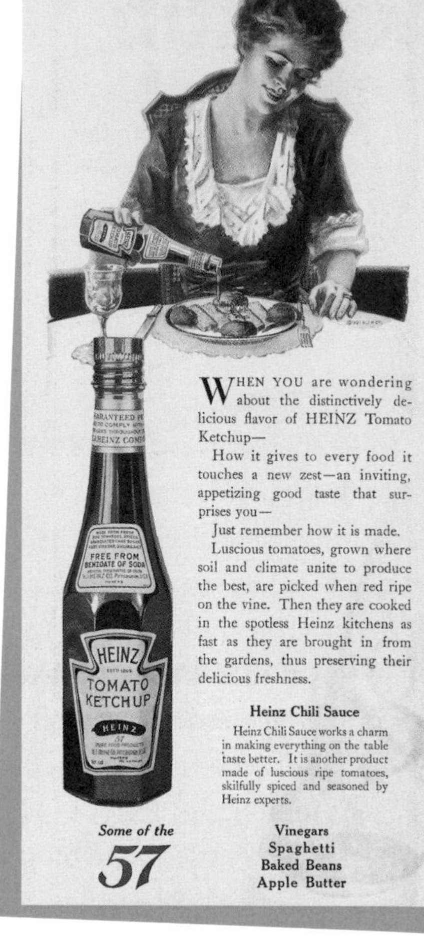

had to be peeled, slowly boiled, and the paste continually stirred.

Early ketchup bottles had corks instead of metal caps.

In 1876, Henry Heinz, a German-American chef, entered the ketchup picture. People liked the sauce, but they sure didn't like all the work involved in making it. When Heinz offered the first mass-produced bottled ketchup, homemakers eagerly bought it. It came in a wide-based, thin-necked bottle—and was just as hard to get out then as it is today!

Mayonnaise is named after Mahón, the port city of the island of Minorca. Originally a visiting Frenchman called it "sauce of Mahón." The French renamed it *mahonnaise*, a spelling that was changed by Americans to *mayonnaise*.

Before making a splash with ketchup, starting back in 1869, Henry Heinz produced a wide variety of other bottled or canned fruits, vegetables, and sauces. As the years passed, he kept coming out with an ever-increasing number of new products. One day in 1892, while riding an elevated train through New York, Heinz spotted a sign above a store that read 21 STYLES OF SHOES. Suddenly inspired, he created his own slogan: 57 VARIETIES. At the time, the company actually produced sixty-five different products. Henry Heinz didn't care; he simply liked the way the number 57 looked in print.

On Tomato Ketchup:
If you do not shake the bottle,
None'll come, and then a lot'll.
—Anonymous

Leotard

21

Jules Léotard was in love . . . with himself.

The nineteenth-century French circus acrobat was known for his good looks, his vanity, and for his feats of skill on the trapeze. He caused a sensation in circuses and theaters by flying from one trapeze to another, often right over the heads of the spectators. Léotard was also the first to do an aerial somersault. He would swing out on the trapeze, let go, do a complete flip in the air, then catch hold of another trapeze. After perfecting the trick, he predicted that all emulators would break their necks (an unfounded fear).

Léotard was only twenty-one at the height of his fame. He devised many of his acts while practicing on ropes and rings suspended above the swimming pool at his father's gymnasium.

Etching of nineteenth-century trapeze artists

Later in his career, Léotard wrote a book about his favorite subject: himself. The little volume begins with an account of his infancy. During this time, according to the author, only being hung upside down from a trapeze bar could stop his crying. "Which is why I grew up to be the world's greatest trapeze artist," he modestly added.

The safety net for circus performers was introduced in 1871 by a traveling acrobatic troupe, the Flying Rizarellis.

Near the end of the book, Léotard talks about the clothing he wore when performing. Convinced that he had about the best-looking body of any man who ever existed, he always performed in a one-piece, sleeveless, tight-fitting garment to show off his physique.

Today we call the item a leotard.

The vain acrobat is long since gone—but not forgotten. He would be pleased to know that he has been immortalized as a word.

When he didn't have access to his father's pool, Léotard relied on a pile of mattresses on the floor to break his fall when he practiced.

Léotard was also immortalized in a popular song of the time "That Daring Young Man on the Flying Trapeze."

Liquid Paper®

22

The date: December 1951. The place: A bank in Dallas, Texas.

Bette Nesmith Graham, a secretary, was happily typing away. That's when it happened—she made a mistake!

Back in those days, before computers, people used typewriters with a carbon-film ribbon. The only way to get rid of typing goof-ups was with an eraser, which more often than not just left a black, smudgy splotch.

Bette Graham was a poor typist, especially when using a newfangled contraption of the 1950s, the electric typewriter.

While erasing her mistake (and making a mess in the process) Bette's glance happened to fall on a pair of holiday-window painters who were brushing over smudges and flaws in their work. She suddenly had a great idea: why couldn't a similar technique be used to correct typing mistakes?

During the sixties, Michael Nesmith, Bette's son, made a name for himself as a member of the rock group the Monkees.

The next day, Bette showed up for work with a small bottle of white tempera paint (and other ingredients) and a little watercolor brush. Soon her coworkers were asking for bottles of their own. All the requests led to another idea—starting her own business.

Mistake Out. That's what Bette called her product at first. Within a couple of years she had a thriving business going in her garage, with her son Michael as her right-hand man. Together they filled up 150 bottles of Mistake Out every month.

In 1956, Bette decided to patent her product and trademark the name, which she and Michael changed to Liquid Paper. Shortly after an article about Bette and her invention appeared in a national magazine, sales skyrocketed.

In 1968, the Liquid Paper Company was producing up to 10,000 bottles a year; by the mid-seventies, the figure was up to 25 million annually. In 1978, Bette sold the company to The Gillette Company for $47 million.

By 1975, Liquid Paper was being sold in thirty-one countries.

The sales and use of computers have steadily risen; as a result, those of Liquid Paper and other brands of correction fluid have steadily declined.

It is illegal to use correction fluid on official documents such as police records, birth certificates, and medical records.

Makeup

Although Cleopatra lived more than two thousand years ago, even in her time the use of cosmetics was widespread. In fact, the famous queen wrote a short book on the subject. It discussed the use of creams, nail polish, perfumes, skin colorings, and lipstick.

Long before Cleopatra, people around the globe were painting their bodies and faces. Incan women wore lipstick and darkened their eyebrows with black greasepaint. The ancient people of Caledonia, now Scotland, covered their bodies with elaborate designs, using a blue pigment. Men and women of the Middle East colored their fingernails, the palms of their hands, and even the soles of their feet with henna, a dark red dye. In Egypt, eyeliner was the most important. Made from ground ants' eggs and a black paste, it was applied by both men and women to their eyelashes, lids, and brows.

Although the word *cosmetics* comes from the Greek *kosmētikos* (meaning "skilled in adornment"), the Greeks frowned on the use of makeup and considered it a sign of bad character. The Romans did, too, until Nero, one of the most peculiar Roman emperors, started appearing in public with his face all colorfully made up—to match his wife's.

Isabeau, a queen of France during the fourth century, wanted to have softer, prettier skin. To achieve this, she daily smeared her hands and face with a special lotion. The lotion was a mixture of pig brains, crocodile glands, and wolf blood.

The most ancient cosmetic is lipstick. Today, more than $1 billion is spent on lipstick a year.

In Western Europe, only the ruling class could afford expensive, imported cosmetics. Ordinary people whitened their skin with flour and colored their lips and cheeks with beet juice.

In Europe, during the seventeenth century, both men and women wore "beauty patches" to cover smallpox scars. Made of black silk or velvet, they were in the shape of dots, stars, and hearts. As many as a dozen might be worn at a time.

By the 1500s, the French and English had become notorious for the huge amount of makeup they wore. "People haveth come to looke quite unreal, and hardley like people at all," wrote one commentator of the times. On occasion, men and women painted their faces with a mixture of gold leaf and hot lemon juice. Other times, they whitened their faces with rice powder and etched their facial veins in blue. Worse yet was a short-lived fad of painting one's face with white lead. Little by little, people realized how poisonous lead was; as it seeped into the bloodstream through the skin, it caused horrible scarring, baldness, and, in some cases, even death.

In eighteenth-century Europe, people took to shaving off their eyebrows and attaching fake ones of mouse skin.

While it's true that people have sometimes gotten carried away with their makeup, they have also gone to the other extreme. Among American Puritans during the sixteenth century, it was against the law to wear makeup of any sort. Doing so was considered vain, sluttish, and "an abomination before the eyes of God." For this "crime," a woman could be whipped, held underwater until she was half dead, or put in prison. Also, wearing makeup was grounds for divorce. All the man had to do was go into court and tattle on his wife, and the marriage was over.

Margarine

In 1869 in France, butter was in short supply and too expensive for most people. France was getting ready for war with Prussia and needed a butter substitute that would store well on ships.

After mulling over the situation, Emperor Napoleon III decided to have a contest to see who could come up with the most "suitable substance to replace butter for the navy and the less prosperous classes."

Only one person entered the contest—Hippolyte Mège-Mouriés. The final result of his experiments took the form of a compound of animal fat, skim milk, pig's stomach, cow's udder, and bicarbonate of soda. At one stage in the process it had the appearance of a string of pearls, so the inventor called it *margarine*—from the Greek word *margaron*, meaning "pearl."

Instead of animal fats, modern margarine in the U.S. is made using *vegetable* fats—such as soybean, peanut, or corn oil. Gone are cows' udders and pigs' stomachs from the list of ingredients!

Often added to the list are vitamins D and A. And some brands use softeners to make it easier to spread.

Margarine is naturally white. A few months after it was

In European countries, whale oil was once widely used to make margarine. That changed during the second half of the twentieth century with the passage of laws to protect whales.

Two brothers opened the world's first margarine factory in Holland in 1871.

By law, manufacturers couldn't dye their margarine yellow, but people could do it on their own. This led to the creation of margarine-making kits like the Delrich E-Z Color Pak, at right. This 1948 ad tells you how easy it is. First, you "pinch" your "color berry," then "knead the bag"—and presto! Just like that, you've got gobs of golden margarine!

In England, margarine was first called Butterine.

invented, manufacturers began adding yellow dye to make it look more appetizing and more like butter.

Dairymen didn't like all the sudden, new competition with butter—one of their most important products. They banded together and did everything possible to destroy the fledgling margarine industry. Incredibly, they were able to get laws passed in the 1880s that made it illegal to dye margarine yellow! It took over seventy years to get these laws repealed; not until the 1950s was the last of them stricken from the law books.

Napkin

25

If you were an ancient Egyptian, Greek, or Roman and you were invited over to someone's home for dinner, this is what you could expect: the meal would last for hours, and it would be super-messy—because all the diners would be eating with their hands. For this reason, each person would have a huge napkin—one as big as a full-size towel. Also available would be finger bowls of water scented with herbs, rose petals, or orange blossoms.

During the sixth century B.C., the Romans came up with a second use for the napkin (and invented something else we use today): the doggie bag. Guests were expected to wrap uneaten food in their napkins and take it home with them. To leave empty-handed was considered really bad manners.

The invention of the fork did away with towel-sized napkins. Since people were no longer eating with their hands, only small napkins, like those we use today, were needed.

Even after the coming of the modern-sized napkin, most Europeans—especially the English—did not use them. Instead, their custom was to use the tablecloth. The edge of the tablecloth was always draped over one's lap—and was intended as a hand-wipe as well as a means of protecting against spills. (For

In seventeenth-century Italy, napkins were folded into all sorts of fancy shapes. For a young woman, it was in the shape of a chick; a hen shape was for a woman of the highest rank; that for a priest was in the shape of Noah's ark; bears, ducks, and bunnies were for kids.

A book on etiquette published in England in 1729 suggests: "When the fingers are very greasy, wipe them first on a piece of bread, in order not to soil the [napkin] too much."

This etching of an English man and woman shows a tablecloth being used as a napkin.

this reason, the original meaning of the English word *napkin* is "tablecloth.")

The doily was invented in England by a tailor named Doily. Originally the items were referred to as "Doily's napkins" and were used during the serving of dessert.

Serviette or *naperon*—those are the two names the French used for the item. The English, borrowing on *naperon*, created two words: *napkin*, a small cloth for the lap; and *apron*, the garment protecting the cook's clothing.

Parking Meters

26

They're ugly. Nobody likes them. They take your money. In return, they give you something that used to be free.

The parking meter was the brainchild of Carlton Magee, the editor in chief of a leading Oklahoma City newspaper. In 1933, the mayor of the city set up a Businessman's Traffic Committee "to inquire into methods of imposing stricter parking controls in our town." Magee was elected chairman of the group.

In 1975 in Carson City, Nevada, a man named Harold Hess received a parking ticket even though he showed the meter maid that the meter was frozen. "Not my problem," she told him. The next day he paid the ticket—handing the cashier at the county courthouse a block of ice with the money and ticket frozen inside it. "Hey! How am I supposed to get that out?" demanded the cashier. Hess just shrugged. "Not my problem," he said as he walked out.

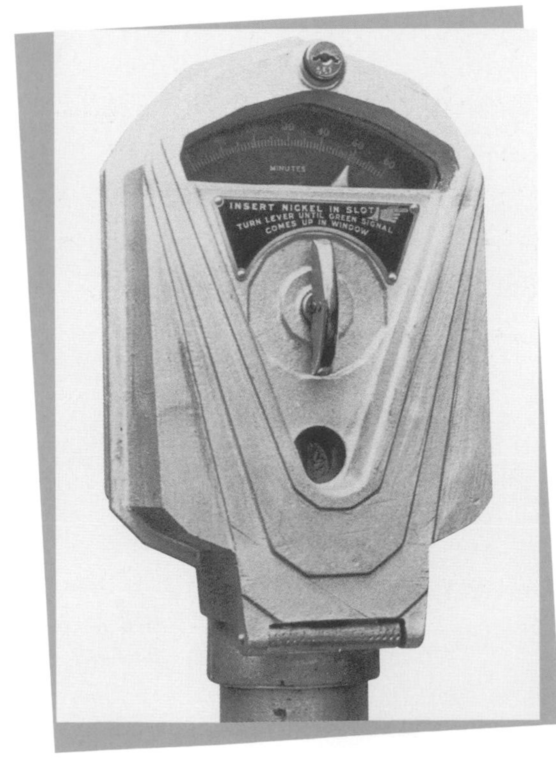

First installed parking meter, Oklahoma City, 1935

Woman inserting a coin in parking meter (1930s)

Magee was no dummy. First he came up with the idea of the parking meter, and then he figured out how to make one. Basically, he took the idea of the vending machine: put a coin in a machine, turn the crank, and out comes gum or candy. But with Magee's machines, there was one big difference: nothing came out. No gum, no candy. Just time to leave your car somewhere until you either fed the meter more money—or got a parking ticket.

Magee started his own company, making the first-ever parking meters (which looked like the heads of metal Martians). The city immediately ordered 150 units, and on July 16, 1935, the first parking meters went into service.

"Smart" parking meters are now coming into use. Electronic sensors in the pavement determine how long a car has been in one spot. When the allotted time is up, the meter won't accept any more coins.

Parking meters are being designed to accept (or reject!) credit cards.

The Duncan Toy Company (best known for its yo-yos) is presently the leading manufacturer of parking meters in the United States!

Traffic officer removing the money from a parking meter (1930s)

Photocopier

27

The year was 1903. George Beidler, working at an Oklahoma City land-claim office, was getting really sick of his job. The worst part was the need for constant duplication of legal documents, which had to be retyped or laboriously copied by hand. There had to be a better way, he decided.

After four long years, Beidler came out with a soon-to-be-forgotten device called the Rectigraph, which, all in all, worked on the same basic principles as a camera. The thing was big, slow, produced very poor copies, and required a large team of experts just to make it work at all.

People gave up on the idea of ever making a photocopier.

Then one hot summer day in 1937, the residents of an apartment building in Queens, New York, started griping—and holding their noses. A terrible stink was coming from the apartment of a man named Chester Carlson.

Carlson apologized. He was working on an experiment, he explained, and one of the chemicals he had to use was sulfur (which has the lovely aroma of rotten eggs). His neighbors demanded that he abandon his stinky project. Politely, he refused. And went back to working on his photocopying machine.

Photocopying was first called xerography, which comes from two Greek words—*xēros* for "dry" and *graphein* for "writing." Now it is frequently referred to as xeroxing.

The first fully automatic Xerox machine was called the 914.

Chester F. Carlson with his prototype photocopying machine

Xerox was the first company to develop the idea of the personal computer, but various problems at the time prevented it from successfully marketing the product.

In 1876, Thomas Edison invented the mimeograph machine, a device that used a "wet" ink copying process—a precursor to the later photographic processes. It was like a very small printing press for use in homes, schools, and offices.

It wasn't at all like the Rectigraph. It was smaller, utilized a different process—and, most important, it worked. His first patent was filed in April 1939, and he followed this with a patent for an automatic machine in November 1940.

With dollar signs in his eyes, certain he had come up with something fantastic, Carlson went from company to company, trying to get them interested in mass-producing his machine. Incredibly, no one was interested!

Ten years passed. Finally, Carlson demonstrated his photocopier for a small family-owned firm, the Haloid Company. They were impressed. Today the Haloid Company is the Xerox Corporation, one of the largest manufacturers of business machines in the world.

Post-it® Notes

28

A flop. A failure. An experiment that didn't work. And then making the best out of a bad thing. That's how Post-it Notes came to be.

One day in 1974, Arthur Fry, a chemist, was hard at work at his job at 3M (Minnesota Manufacturing and Mining Company), best known for its manufacture of Scotch tape. Nearby, a colleague was grumbling and complaining. All week, Fry's fellow worker had been trying to develop a super-strong adhesive; instead, he produced a super-weak one.

Post-its now come in an extremely wide variety of colors and styles, including dark colors that you write on using light-colored ink.

"Look at this gunk," he groused to Fry. "This stuff never dries. It won't even hold two pieces of paper together—at least not permanently."

Fry nodded. All he could do was commiserate and tell his friend to keep trying.

The following Sunday, Fry was at church, singing in the choir. He was getting annoyed: the slips of paper he used to mark his place in his hymnal kept falling out. As the service continued and the minister delivered the sermon, Fry was suddenly inspired—but not in a religious way. He thought of his colleague's extra-weak adhesive and realized it would be perfect for keeping book markers in place.

Inventor Arthur Fry with a Post-it Note on his forehead

Today there are even digital Post-its that you can "stick" in a computer document as reminders to yourself.

The next day at work, Fry made a stack of small, square-shaped notepaper. Across the top of each he applied a thin layer of the adhesive, then pressed them together into a pad. One problem: when the notes were peeled off, they sometimes left a sticky residue. After days of fiddling with the formula for the adhesive, he solved the problem. Soon he was passing out samples to his coworkers at 3M.

Advertisements printed on Post-it Notes are now getting stuck on daily newspapers. Readers notice them more than other ads because they stand out.

A short time later, Fry was writing a report and had a question about a piece of information. He wrote the question on one of his markers and attached it to the report, with an arrow pointing to the information. Fry's manager at 3M, Bob Molenda, wrote his answer on the bottom of the note and attached it to an item he was returning. It was during a coffee break that afternoon when the two men suddenly realized that what Fry had devised was not just a marker but also a new way to communicate and organize information. Self-attaching notes!

Soon Fry's colleagues were using the item the same way and asking him for more of the notepads. At that point, Fry came to the realization that his little self-attaching notes were a very useful and salable product.

Fry's boss agreed. A few months later, Post-it Notes were popping up all over the United States—and then in other countries as well.

Rubber Hats, Coats, and Boots

29

In the early 1800s, people tried making all sorts of products out of rubber. None were much good—for the reason that extremes in temperature completely changed the substance. In the winter, rubber coats froze stiff as boards, then cracked and fell apart. In the summer, rubber boots turned soft, gooey, and smelly. They stank so much that people had to bury them!

Charles Goodyear believed he could solve the problem. But he was desperately poor—so poor that he was in and out of jail most of his life for not paying his bills. When not in jail, he lived with his wife and children in a shack in Connecticut. The Goodyear family was often sick and without money for food, clothing, or fuel. They foraged in fields to find wood for the winter. They begged for food and medicine from neighbors. The children dug half-grown potatoes out of other people's gardens.

Meanwhile, Charles Goodyear had some success in his makeshift lab in the kitchen of his shack. In 1835, he won medals at fairs for inventing a rubber life raft and a large number of other all-rubber items. Unfortunately, though improved, the rubber still did not stand up well enough to extremes of temperature.

The substance that Goodyear discovered in his kitchen was originally referred to as "India rubber" because it was first used by the "Indians" of what is now Mexico and Central and South America. In the nineteenth century, Goodyear used heat and sulfur to "vulcanize" rubber; 3,500 years earlier, the Mayans were using solar heat and juice from morning glory vines (which contains sulfur) to achieve the same end.

Goodyear was criticized for not taking proper care of his family. He even sold his children's schoolbooks so he could continue with his experiments.

Goodyear made a bit of money selling an item now and then, but never enough. He had little more than the clothes—the rubber clothes—on his back. He wore a cap, coat, and shoes—all made of rubber. His wife and daughters wore rubber bonnets and carried rubber purses. Even some of the furniture in his run-down home was made of rubber.

One icy February evening in 1839, during an experiment, Goodyear was trying to "cure" rubber using various chemicals. Accidentally, he spilled a mixture of sulfur and rubber onto the hot surface of his stove. There it melted, then eventually cooled and solidified. When he later got around to scooping it up, he was startled to find how smooth, dry, and flexible it was. That night, in numbing winter cold, he nailed the pancake-sized slab of the stuff outside the kitchen door. In the morning, he let out a whoop of triumph: the rubber was not brittle. It was strong, flexible, and elastic.

Goodyear continued working on his inventions even while in debtors' prison, getting supplies for his experiments from friends and sympathetic jailers.

In 1844, Charles Goodyear received a patent for what he called "vulcanized rubber." Using his invention, manufacturers began making all sorts of new products—rubber coats, hats, and boots, to name a few. Because Goodyear held the patent, some companies paid him (as they were supposed to), but most never gave him a cent. At the age of sixty, he died as he had lived—in abject poverty.

Goodyear did not make tires, but it was his invention of vulcanization that made the manufacture of rubber tires possible. A number of rubber companies are named in his honor, including the Goodyear Tire & Rubber Company.

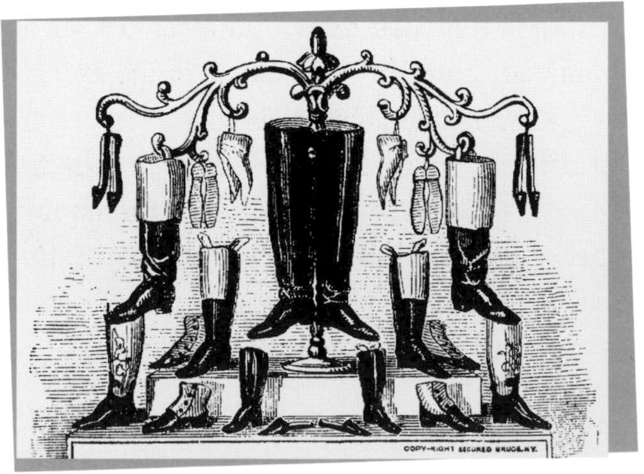

This strange nineteenth-century engraving shows a whole array of rubber footwear

Safety Pin

Fifteen dollars started it all.

The year was 1825. Walter Hunt, an inventor living in New York, was in debt for fifteen dollars—a lot of money in those days. But Hunt didn't have a nickel to his name. He lived in a shabby apartment. He could hardly pay the rent, and there was never enough food on the table. So how was he supposed to come up with all that cash?

The Sumerians, an ancient people of the Middle East, were the first to fashion iron straight pins.

The man to whom Hunt owed the money had a weird idea. Knowing that Hunt was an inventor, he handed him a piece of wire.

"Invent something," he told Hunt. "I'll give you four hundred dollars for the rights to anything worthwhile you can make out of it."

Because of a shortage of straight pins in the late Middle Ages, Britain passed a law allowing the selling of pins only on certain days of the year.

For over three hours, Hunt fiddled with the wire. An idea gradually began to take shape in his mind, and as it did, the wire took shape in his hands.

The next day Hunt gave the wire back to the man, only he had turned it into something else: the safety pin. For his invention, Hunt made four hundred dollars, minus the fifteen-dollar debt. The other man made a fortune.

One last twist: Hunt did not invent the safety pin. Though

he may not have known it, the device had already been invented. Almost four thousand years before he was born, the ancient Greeks and Romans had been using safety pins to hold their togas together!

In A.D. 1200, people began using buttons to fasten clothes instead of safety pins. Soon buttons had replaced safety pins as clothes fasteners to such a great extent that the pins became almost extinct.

Walter Hunt's pin was stronger and springier. And it was also safer: unlike those of ancient times, its point, when closed, was always completely covered.

Hunt pursued a career as an inventor the rest of his life. He created an improved ice plow, a nail-making machine, and a repeating rifle. But none of these were completely original ideas; all had been made before. Mr. Hunt's talent, it seems, was not in thinking up new, surprising inventions; rather, it was in making old ones better.

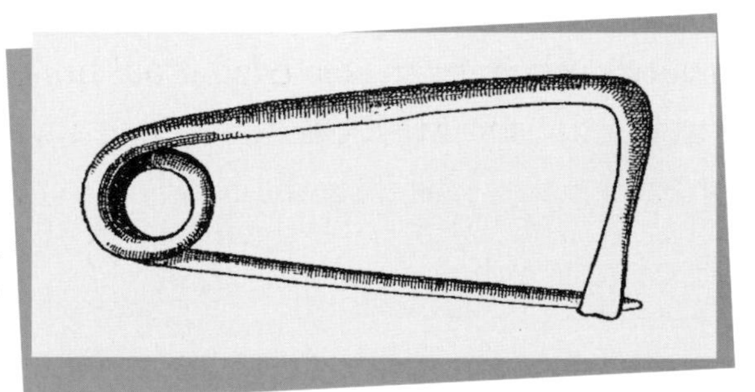

The safety pin shown here was probably used by the ancient Greeks four thousand years ago.

Snowboard

Snowboarding is one of the newest, youngest sports. Its inventor was pretty young, too.

In 1963, Tom Sims was an eighth-grader at a New Jersey middle school. One day in his wood shop class, Tom suddenly had an idea. A week later he had created a contraption he called a "ski board." Ridden sideways like a skateboard, it looked like a very short, fat ski. Tom tried it out on local hills; it worked great. He did spins through the air and carved high-

More people throughout the United States ski than snowboard—about a four-to-one ratio.

Skiing injuries dropped 26 percent between 1993 and 1997, mostly because of better equipment, while snowboarding injuries tripled. According to experts, this is because too many snowboarders do not wear helmets and sometimes do foolish, daredevil stunts.

Kari White cuts across a snowy hill on her snowboard.

speed turns through the snow. Extremely pleased with its performance, Tom made more, many of which had foot straps. Eventually, Tom formed a company to manufacture his invention. Snowboarding was born!

There were twenty-three snowboarding deaths in the United States between 1991 and 1999, most as the result of head, neck, and spinal injuries. Be careful!

Three years later, another young man, Sherman Poppen, patented the "Snurfer"—which consisted of two skis bolted together. There were no metal edges or foot straps; however, it *did* have a rein tied to its front tip for steering. The Snurfer became the first mass-produced version of the snowboard, retailing for fifteen dollars. Today a top-of-the-line snowboard can cost five hundred dollars or more.

There are now millions of snowboarders—and more people are trying the sport every day. In 1998 snowboarding made its debut in the Winter Olympics.

It all started because a kid in a shop class had an idea.

The snowboard evolved from the skateboard. The skateboard, invented by surfers, first became popular during the 1950s. It consisted of a board and the wheels from two roller skates. Called "sidewalk surfers," skateboards really took off in the 1960s when American Frank Nasworthy began mass-producing what he called "Cadillac wheels."

Rider Shaun White, totally airborne on his snowboard!

Snowmobile

32

During the 1800s, people started thinking about how to invent a dogless dogsled—one powered by something other than "man's best friend." Most of these early efforts were rather pathetic. One was a huge toboggan with a sail attached—which, of course, didn't go anywhere at all when there wasn't enough wind. Another used a hand crank as its source of power; turning the crank made toothed wooden wheels go around. Last (and probably least) was a contraption that used foot pedals connected by iron rods to a paddle wheel at the back.

Worldwide, twenty thousand snowmobiles are sold annually.

In the 1890s, inventors started tinkering with the idea of a car that could be driven across the snow. But nobody could make one that worked—not until 1923. In that year, Virgil White of New Hampshire invented a kit that could convert a Model T Ford into a vehicle for traveling over the snow. White patented the name "snowmobile."

In the United States, over 4 million people have ridden a snowmobile at least once.

Four years later, Wisconsin native Carl Eliason built a super-long sled with an engine mounted on the front that turned two loops of heavy chain along each side. Eliason gradually improved the design by making the sled out of metal, moving the engine to the rear, and adding a windshield to protect the driver.

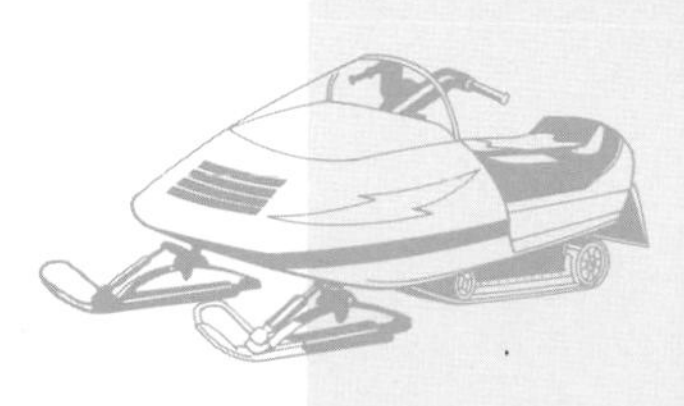

Bombardier's prototype snowmobile, with propeller and Model T Ford engine

During the same time period, Joseph-Armand Bombardier, a fifteen-year-old Canadian, was hard at work on a similar idea. Ultimately, he devised a vehicle that was far superior to Eliason's machine and to White's kit for converting a car during the winter months. Bombardier's vehicle was designed exclusively for the snow. Far more than any other person, it is young Mr. Bombardier who should be credited with the invention of the snowmobile.

Some modern snowmobiles reach speeds of up to one hundred miles per hour.

Bombardier's creation consisted of a Model T Ford frame with four sleigh runners (borrowed from the family sled!); the engine from the same Model T powered a large, hand-carved propeller. While he operated the engine controls, his little brother Léopold steered the runners with his feet.

Worried about the danger, the kids' dad ordered them to scrap the invention. An argument led to a compromise: the boys could keep working on the project on the condition that they get rid of the propeller—the most dangerous part.

Joseph-Armand went to work—and kept at it for almost twenty years. Finally, in 1940, he achieved real commercial success by building a tractorlike vehicle for the snow. It was fully enclosed, powered by a V-8 Ford engine, and had four large wheels on each side. The vehicle sold well all over the world. It could carry twelve passengers—or several hundred pounds of supplies—and was used for everything from hauling wood to carrying mail to transporting students in rural communities.

In some remote, snowbound parts of the world, snowmobiles are the main form of transportation. This is true, for example, in certain regions of Finland.

It may have been a big snow vehicle that got Bombardier going, but it was a little one that made him rich and famous. In 1957 he developed a small sled he called the Ski-Doo Snowmobile. It had a 7.5-horsepower engine in front and moved along on twin rubber tracks rotated by toothed gears. What made the two-passenger vehicle special was its light weight and speed (thirty-five miles per hour). It sold well from the start, and sales skyrocketed in 1959 when it was redesigned to include two "steering skis" in front.

Since then, dozens of different brands have been introduced. All are based on the design of the original Ski-Doo Snowmobile.

Stereo

Invented in Germany in 1881 by Clement Ader, the first-ever stereo system was totally weird. Here's how it worked:

For a fee, subscribers had a telephone-like contraption installed in their homes. At a set time, music was transmitted over ordinary telephone lines. To listen to it, a person held two telephone receivers, one to each ear. Half the music came through one receiver, half through the other.

Not until 1925 was stereo music broadcast via radio rather than telephone.

The first stereophonic phonographs and records were introduced in 1958. CDs, which became commercially available in 1982, were stereophonic from the start.

Two men listening to a stereo broadcast

Engraving of an early Walkman-like stereo receiver

The music was always "live"—an opera, symphony, or other musical performance. At the theater where it was taking place, two groups of microphones were set up on either side of the stage, and these relayed the music to people's homes.

This early type of stereophonic listening seems pretty strange—especially the two-earphones part. But if you think about it, a similar device is still used (and very popular) today! You may even own one—and now you know that the Walkman is a throwback to the very first type of stereo.

Before stereo, voices, noises, and music in movies came at the viewer from the front. With stereo soundtracks, it comes from everywhere—from behind, in front, beside, and above the viewer. The first stereophonic soundtrack accompanied Walt Disney's *Fantasia* in 1940.

Stockings

Matted, stitched-together animal fur—that is what the first stockings were made from! Called *piloi*, these hairy socks were mentioned by the Greek poet Hesiod in 8 B.C.

The Romans considered it unmanly for men to wear stockings. Stockings, they believed, were only for women.

In the fourth century, the Catholic Church adopted above-the-knee stockings of white linen for priests.

The Romans wrapped their feet, ankles, and legs with long strips of cloth or leather. Later came *udones*, which were a lot like modern socks. Two pieces of cloth were cut into a foot-shaped pattern and then sewn together. Because they were made of material that didn't stretch, the things fit poorly and sagged sloppily down around the ankles.

It was the Egyptians who solved this problem. They invented knitted socks, which were more elastic and fit much more snugly. Hand-knitted socks discovered in tombs in Egypt have been dated between the third and sixth centuries B.C.

The art of making knitted socks quickly spread across Europe. In 1589, an English preacher invented a sock-knitting machine. The machine was so perfect in its design that it continued to be the only mechanical means of producing knitted socks for over 250 years.

Before 1900, 99 percent of all women's stockings were made of cotton or wool. By 1929, the situation had been reversed, and 99 percent were made of silk or rayon (artificial silk). In 1939, nylons (made of a synthetic fiber) hit the scene—and silk and rayon took a permanent hike.

During World War II, nylon was diverted to the war effort, where it was used to make parachutes, mosquito netting, blood filters, and sutures. Nylon stockings became very hard to get, which led to one of the strangest stocking fads of all time: women in the United States began painting their legs to look

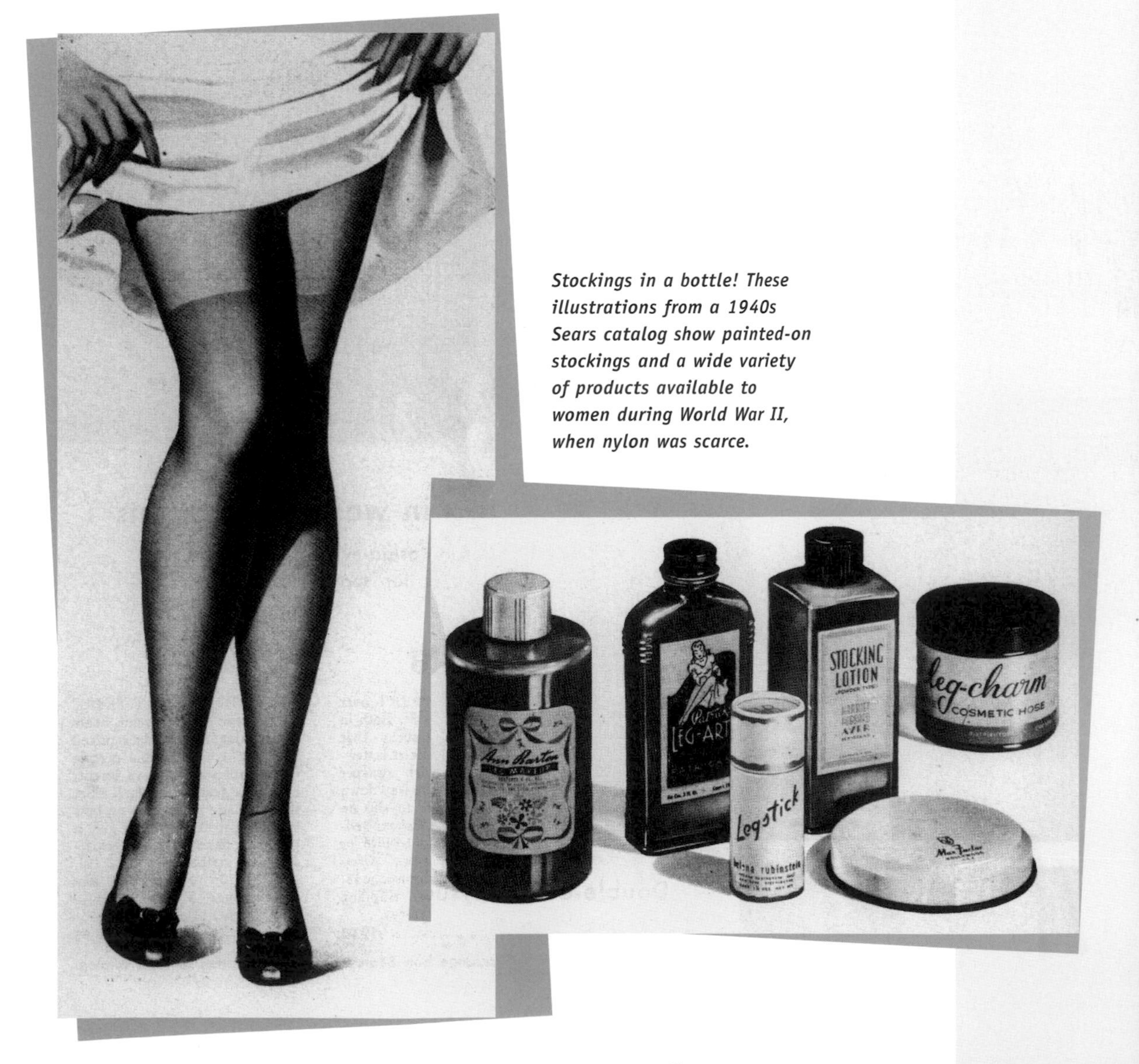

Stockings in a bottle! These illustrations from a 1940s Sears catalog show painted-on stockings and a wide variety of products available to women during World War II, when nylon was scarce.

Fourteenth-century Italian youths wore short jackets and ragged tights, usually with each leg a different color.

Nylon is almost inflammable.

as though they were wearing nylons! The special paint came in small cans that included instructions about how to paint seams. With the end of the war in 1945 came many blessings, among them the switch from painted-on stockings to real ones.

Until the 1960s, tight, itchy garter belts with all sorts of dangling doodads and annoying snaps and fasteners held up nylon stockings. One day in 1959, a woman named Ethel Gant was complaining to her husband, Allen, about the discomfort of having to wear a garter belt to hold up her nylons. Allen Gant, the president of a textile company, Glen Raven Mills of North Carolina, suddenly had an idea. Excited, he told Ethel his idea and asked what she thought of it.

"I think it's great!" she told him.

A few months later the company brought out Panti-Legs, the first-ever "pantyhose"—stockings that cover the body from the waist down. Within a few years, sales for thigh-high nylons were really slipping, while those for pantyhose kept going up and up.

Surfboard

Hawaii—that's where the surfboard was invented. When European explorers first "discovered" the islands in 1778, they found that the people used surfboards for sport, for fishing, and for traveling short distances. Hawaiian boards were solid wood, weighed from sixty to one hundred pounds, and were often up to sixteen feet long. By comparison, modern boards

The highest wave ever ridden by a surfer was fifty feet. In 1868 in Hawaii, a surfer found a fifty-foot tidal wave coming at him—and successfully rode it in order to save his life.

Tom Blake was a leader in the revival of the ancient sport of surfing. This 1924 photo shows him in Hawaii with his collection of handmade boards. Blake patented the hollow surfboard and was the first to fit a surfboard with a fin.

Young ladies riding early surfboards off the coast of South Africa in the early 1900s

are made of fiberglass, weigh from eight to fifteen pounds, and are often only about ten feet in length.

They called themselves the Pendletones. Not until they heard their first song on the radio did they discover that the rcord company had renamed them the Beach Boys.

In 1959, Hawaii became our fiftieth state, and by the early 1960s, a surfing craze swept the country. Its starting point was California. Not only is California the closest state to Hawaii, it has hundreds of miles of coastline—and the best surfing on the U.S. mainland. It also didn't hurt that the country's music and movie industries were already established in the Los Angeles area.

The first surfer "flick" was the film *Gidget*, which gave the sport national exposure in 1959. *Wipe Out, Surfer Girl, Where the Boys Are*, and countless other such movies soon followed. The picture they painted was of an endless summer filled with romance, fun, and the search for the perfect wave. Kids ruled; parents always stayed in the background, quietly baffled by it all.

At first, real surfers didn't like the Beach Boys. Their songs brought out too many "gremmies" (beginners) and "hodads" (fake surfers) who crowded up the beaches.

The Beach Boys offered up the first and, arguably, the best surfer music. Five cool surfers singing about the life they loved: that was the image—and sound—they presented to the world. The fact is that only one of them—Dennis Wilson—could surf at all!

In 1961, songwriter Murray Wilson arranged for his three teenage sons, his nephew, and one of their friends to record a folk song. It didn't impress anybody. But the producer asked them if they had written any original songs. They hadn't, but Dennis said that surf music was starting to get popular in Los Angeles, despite the fact that none of the songs had any lyrics. Surfers had their own language: "Why not use it in a song?" suggested Wilson. Everyone agreed. And right there in the studio they made a list of surfing terms; then, together with the producer, they wrote a song: "Surfin'." It made the charts (#75 nationally). Thirty-four songs followed, fourteen of which were top-ten hits, including three number-ones: "Good Vibrations," "Kokomo," and "Help Me, Rhonda."

The craze is over. Surfer music isn't hot anymore; surfing movies are only on late-night TV. But surfing as a sport is going as strong as ever.

The term *hang ten* means to ride a wave with all ten toes curled over the side of the board.

Even though most surfer movies featured "woodies" (vintage station wagons with real wood panels), very few "real" surfers drove them; they drove panel trucks with beds long enough to safely transport their boards.

Tape Recorder

Before the tape recorder was invented, the first recording of a song was made on wax.

When Poulsen began work on what eventually became the telegraphone, what he was trying to invent was the answering machine.

Called the Code-A-Phone, the answering machine was invented in the United States in 1958.

The atomic bomb, the lightbulb, and the credit card have something strange in common. All of them were described in science fiction stories long before they were invented.

The same holds true for the tape recorder. In his book *Mercury*, published in 1641, Bishop John Wilkins described an invention used to preserve sounds—noises, voices, music. The tape could be played back later. To readers of the book, the author's description of "a sound-recording machine" was an interesting fantasy, whimsical and amusing, but certainly not possible.

In 1899, two and a half centuries later, Valdemar Poulsen invented the telegraphone, which recorded sound on a magnetized *steel* tape. It was the forerunner of the tape recorder, as well as today's wide range of audio-recording devices—everything from cassettes to CDs.

This tape recorder of 1934 could hold two miles of tape, which recorded up to thirty-five minutes of sound.

Telescope

Like so many other important inventions, the telescope was invented by accident.

One day in 1608, a Dutch maker of eyeglasses by the name of Hans Lippershey was working in his shop, inspecting eyeglass lenses. He held up a couple to a window. For a moment, the two lenses lined up; and Lippershey found himself looking at the weather vane atop a distant steeple. To his surprise, the weather vane was hugely magnified.

Galileo had a selfish, stingy side. Wanting to keep other astronomers from equaling or surpassing his achievements, he kept many of his findings secret from them and denied them access to needed equipment.

Hearing of this accidental discovery, Galileo Galilei, an Italian inventor (1564–1642), was soon hard at work. He developed the strongest telescope of his era, able to magnify normal vision up to twenty times. Its use led him to understand that the sun—not the Earth—was the center of the universe, a concept totally at odds with the accepted religious beliefs of the time. For writing and talking about his ideas, Galileo was sentenced by rigid religious authorities to spend the rest of his life—eight years—under house arrest.

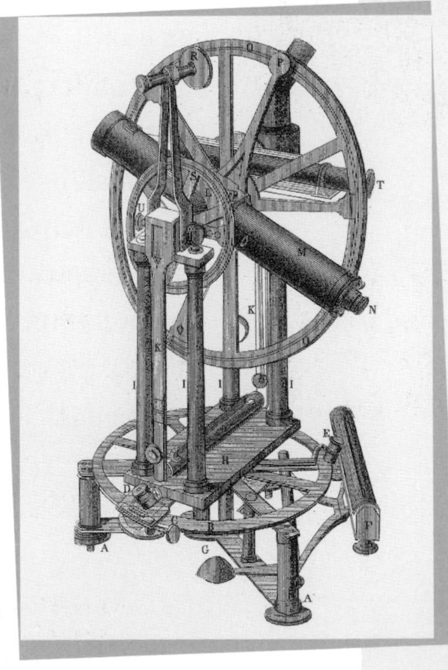

An early telescope

Engraving of a very large nineteenth-century telescope. Notice the playpen-like basket that can be moved up and down the ladder-faced scaffolding. Standing in it, assistants would make adjustments to the telescope when told to do so by the astronomer, who would be peering up through the small end of the scope.

From studying the sun and sunspots, Galileo went blind. Scheiner, his follower, invented a system of using dark glass to protect his eyes, thus saving his sight.

Since its invention, the telescope has constantly been improved upon. In 1611, Galileo was still working to better his version of the device; in the same year, a man named Christoph Scheiner built a telescope that enabled people to see even farther and more clearly. Some fifty years later, Sir Isaac Newton of England made further improvements; as light waves entered the telescope, they were bounced off a small mirror to a larger mirror, which provided an enhanced view.

The radio telescope was developed in the early 1940s. It makes use of the fact that all celestial bodies (suns, planets, moons, et cetera) emit radio waves. A radio telescope is basically a giant "eye" that sees these waves, then amplifies and records them in visual form.

In 1935, a scientist by the name of John Herschel made the shocking announcement that he had invented a telescope so powerful it had enabled him to see people on the moon! Newspapers around the world carried accounts of this amazing scientific breakthrough. A few weeks later, Herschel admitted it had all been nothing but a hoax.

But who knows? Maybe someday we actually *will* have telescopes powerful enough to see creatures on other planets and moons, even those in other solar systems. Come to think of it, maybe these creatures are already watching *us* through *their* telescopes!

Television

People laughed at John Logie Baird. For years, the quiet little Englishman worked in his attic laboratory in London putting together something he called the "televisor." The strange-looking contraption consisted of a tea chest, an empty cookie tin, darning needles, an old electric motor, and lenses from bicycle lights. His electrical supply, which was connected to the motor, consisted of several hundred flashlight batteries wired together to provide a two-thousand-volt source. To the amusement of his friends and neighbors, Baird said he would someday be able to take a picture with a movie camera and relay it directly to the televisor. The picture would appear on the screen and be viewable by spectators.

One cold morning in February of 1924, Baird was ready to test his contraption. At one end of his workroom he focused his little "televisor camera" on a wooden cross. Turning the crank on the camera, he looked over his shoulder at the televisor screen. On it was a shadowy picture of the cross! Though the distance from the camera to the screen was only ten feet, Baird had achieved what, until then, most people had considered impossible.

A few days later Baird tried to duplicate his first success.

In 1925, an editor for a London newspaper, the *Daily Express*, was informed that John Baird was downstairs and wanted to talk with him about his new invention—television. The editor went to an assistant and told him: "For God's sake, go down to reception and get rid of a lunatic who's down there. He says he's got a machine for seeing by wireless [radio]! Watch him! He may have a razor on him!"

Look at this nutty contraption! Hard to believe, but this bunch of junk turned out to be the first workable television. Pictured here is the gizmo's inventor, John Logie Baird.

In 1936, journalist Rex Lambert, confidently and pompously wrote: "Television won't matter in your lifetime or mine."

CBS successfully conducted an experimental color-TV broadcast for the first time in 1941. Ten years later, regular color transmission began with the airing of *The Ed Sullivan Show*: "Live and in color!"

But this time, instead of transmitting a picture, he set off an explosion. His power supply—the hundreds of flashlight batteries—had blown up. No one was hurt, but Baird was evicted by his landlord. As for his televisor, it had been destroyed.

Baird moved to a second-floor apartment a few miles away. Starting from scratch, he reassembled his contraption and continued his experiments. There, on October 30, 1926, he made his greatest breakthrough. Placing a dummy in front of the camera, the inventor began tinkering and fiddling with the televisor, trying to get it to work. Suddenly the dummy's head appeared on the screen!

Thrilled, Baird rushed downstairs in search of a live subject. The first person he encountered was a fifteen-year-old boy, William Taynton. Baird hustled the boy up to his workshop.

"I placed him before the camera-transmitter," wrote Baird, "and went into the next room to see what the televisor would show. The screen was blank. Puzzled and disappointed, I went back to the transmitter, and there the cause of the failure became evident: The boy, scared by the strong light, had backed away from the camera. I gave him some money, and this time he kept his head in the right position. Going again into the next room, I saw his head on the screen quite clearly. It is amusing, I think, that the first person in the world to be seen on [television] needed to be bribed to accept that distinction!"

In 1946, Darryl Zanuck, head of 20th Century-Fox [movie] Studios, wrote: "[Television] won't be able to hold onto any market it captures after the first six months. People will soon get tired of staring at a plywood box every night."

The average American spends an estimated nine years of his/her life watching TV.

Scientists are working on a device that, in case of an emergency such as a tornado, will automatically turn on your television to warn you.

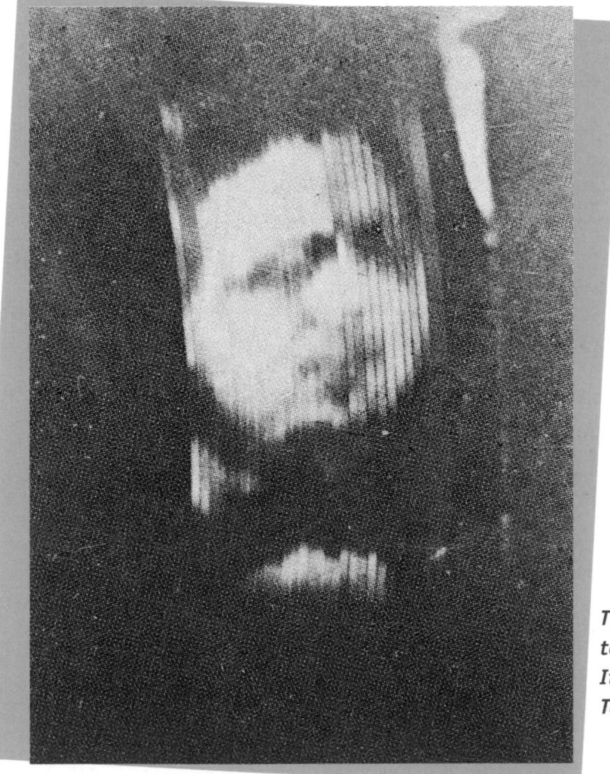

This is one of the first television pictures ever seen. It shows the face of William Taynton, in 1926.

Tires

Imagine you are in England, in the year 1840. You're going biking, so first you check your tires. They are made of *leather*. Not only that, but they're actually *leather garden hoses*—and they're filled with water!

Jump ahead in time a few years. It's 1843, and your bike has what are called "mummy tires." Like earlier "garden hose" tires, they are leather tubes. But instead of water, the tires are filled with grass or horsehair. To protect the leather (and to hold the tire to the wheel), the tires are wrapped, mummylike, around and around with one long strip of canvas.

Some full-size U.S. military submarines have wheels with rubber tires for driving around on the ocean floor! Like the wheels of airplanes, those of submarines are lowered from the vessel's metal belly.

The largest tires are made by the Goodyear Company for mammoth dump trucks. They each are 11 1/2 feet in diameter, weigh 12,500 pounds, and cost $75,000!

Two years later, Englishman Robert Thompson was granted a patent for pneumatic (air-filled) tires. Thompson's tire was an inflatable rubber inner tube enclosed in a canvas sheath. It had a leather outer casing, which consisted of pieces of leather attached to the wheel by metal bolts.

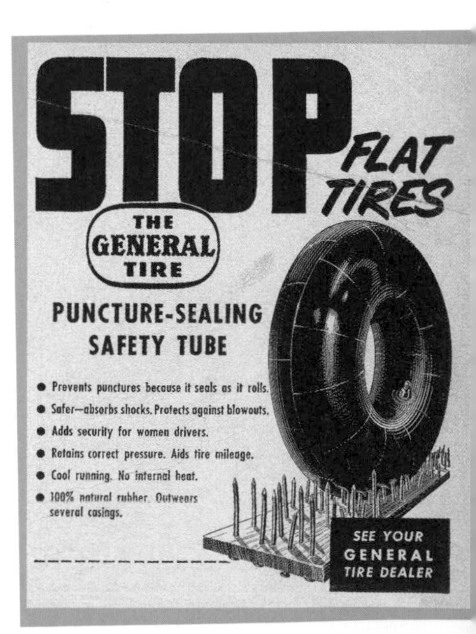

These early tires were for bicy-

A factory worker making mummy tires

cles, tricycles, and carriages. Tires for cars didn't roll around until 1895. Invented by Frenchman Edouard Michelin, they had a hard rubber "outer tire" and a soft rubber inner tube. More than half a century passed before modern "tubeless" tires arrived on the scene. Invented by the B.F. Goodrich Company of Akron, Ohio, such tires form an airtight seal directly with the metal wheel.

Some 250 million tires are discarded annually in the U.S.

Ground rubber "crumbs" from tires can be added to asphalt for paving roads, runways, and playgrounds. Because rubber allows the asphalt to expand and contract when freezing and thawing, adding it to asphalt increases pavement life by at least 400 percent.

Toilet

In the United States, 6.8 billion gallons of water go down the toilet every day. After going through purification facilities, most of the water and human waste end up in the ocean. It's not the greatest system, but it's probably better than most early arrangements for dealing with the problem.

The rulers of ancient Egypt had indoor toilets. Each consisted of a stone seat with a vase below the opening. After the royal business was done, a servant would take the vase away and dump it.

In Rome, some well-to-do people had flush toilets. Water was stored in a tank, and when a valve in the tank was opened, water was released into the toilet bowl. Waste and water then drained down and away through long pipes leading to underground sewers.

They weren't quite so clever in medieval castles in Europe. Set in the thick stone walls—usually in turrets—were privies called garderobes. Beneath a wood or stone toilet seat was a shaft, down which went the waste . . . right into the water-filled moat around the castle! (Just a wild guess, but the moat water probably smelled pretty gross.)

By 1300, towns and cities had begun to spring up all over

In eighteenth-century England, very few homes had running water. Water was available only three days a week, and for only a few hours on those days.

Nineteenth-century London toilets emptied directly into the River Thames. Queen Victoria, on viewing the Thames on one occasion, asked an aide, "What are all those things floating in the river?" Discreetly, the aide replied, "Your Majesty, they are notices that swimming here is forbidden."

This odd-looking toilet from a nineteenth-century plumbing catalog was called the Inodoro. The name is a play on words meaning an O-shaped seat to keep odors in.

In the nineteenth century, carriages often had "carriage pots" built in under the seats. People lifted the seat cushion, sat on a board below it, and relieved themselves into the pot through an opening in the board.

Europe. Usually, people just relieved themselves right in the street, urinating and defecating in corners or behind buildings. There were also outhouses. Public outhouses were usually built on bridges over rivers and streams; private outhouses were attached to the second or third story of a house, overhanging a street or alley.

In every home, various kinds of receptacles were used. The most common was a chamber pot, a container for the bedroom made of ceramic or lightweight metal. Others had an item called a close-stool, a portable, lidded box. The user flipped the lid, sat down on the open seat, and then made a contribution to a removable bowl inside the box. Some close-stools were ornately decorated and had velvet-padded seats.

The first toilet in the White House in 1825 was installed for President John Quincy Adams (leading to a new slang term for a toilet—a *Quincy*).

Naturally, the receptacles had to be emptied. No problem: When done, people would just fling the contents out a window and into the street! They would yell "Loo!" as a warning to passersby before heaving the mess out the window. (For this reason, to this day English people call a toilet a "loo.")

The streets in those times were foul, stinking messes that attracted swarms of flies, rats, and other vermin. Finally, people began to realize that a new system was needed. Thus, instead of tossing their waste into the street, people would leave the pots outside their door. In the morning, workers called "night soil men" would gather up the pots, empty and rinse them in the local stream, then return them to their owners. Fun job!

Credit (or blame) Charles Van Cleave for the pay toilet. In 1910, he invented the coin-operated lock for public toilet stalls.

This kept the streets cleaner. But streams and other watercourses became horribly polluted. Because this was the same water that people drank, deadly diseases repeatedly swept through European towns and cities.

In the United States, Boston's Tremont House boasted of being the first hotel to offer guests indoor baths, flush toilets, and toilet paper. The facilities were all in the cellar.

In 1589, Elizabethan poet John Harington designed the first flush toilet since Roman times. Water was drawn from a tank into the toilet bowl, then flushed into a cesspool below when a handle on the seat was pulled. Only two Harington toilets were ever built—one for the inventor himself, the other for Queen Elizabeth, his godmother. The term *john*, slang for bathroom, was derived from Sir John's name.

In the late eighteenth century, several people worked to improve the toilet. Notably, Englishman Alexander Cummings designed one that featured a small reservoir tank of water mounted high above the toilet bowl and connected to it by a pipe. Pulling a cord released some of the reservoir water, which flowed down the pipe and into the toilet bowl. From there, the water and waste went down into something the inventor called a Stink Trap, an S-shaped arrangement of pipes with a plug "to cut off all communication of smell from [the cesspool] below."

In the 1860s, another Englishman, Thomas Crapper, made further improvements in toilet design. The most important of these was a new kind of metal float, which acted as an automatic shutoff valve for incoming fresh water. Though Mr. Crapper christened his toilet the Valveless Water-Waste Preventer, it soon came to be popularly known by its inventor's last name. Because it was the best toilet of its day, people back then would brag about having a "Crapper" in their home.

Throughout the twentieth century, toilet design continued to improve. Now toilets are going high-tech! And the Japanese are leading the way—creating commodes that do just about everything but paint your toenails. Remote control opens the lid, exposing a comfy, heated seat. The remote regulates the temperature—and also releases odor-masking aromas and camouflaging sounds. When you're finished, a plastic arm swings out from underneath and lets loose a soothing spray of cleansing water. Then sit back and relax as a blow-dryer finishes the job.

Oh, and don't forget to flush. Just tap the remote, and your business is done.

Not until the 1920s did it become common in the U.S. to have separate public bathrooms for males and females. Those for men were called *Johns*. Those for women were called *Janes*, since Jane is the feminine form of the name John.

Los Angeles has the largest sewer system in the U.S. The 65,000-mile-long labyrinth carries 458 million gallons of gunk a day. Most of it goes through a treatment plant, and then it is pumped into the Pacific Ocean.

41 Toilet Paper

In the days before toilet paper, when Americans used corn husks and corncobs, the Japanese used seaweed.

Instead of in rolls, the first toilet paper came in packages of five hundred loose sheets. Advertised as Gayetty's Medicated Papers, it was invented by an American, Joseph Gayetty, in 1857. Mr. Gayetty, it seems, was a rather vain man: to ensure that he would be forever remembered for his contribution to the toilet world, he had his name printed on each sheet!

Gayetty Papers did not sell very well—for two reasons. First, people thought it was wasteful to use clean paper. For free, they could use what they'd always used: corncobs, newspapers, and the pages from old magazines and catalogs. Another reason was that people in those times were very modest. They did not think it was "nice" to think or talk about an item such as toilet paper, and to have been seen purchasing it would have been extremely embarrassing.

The brainchild of Englishman Walter Alcock, Perforated Toilet Tissue Rolls came along in 1879. But the fact that the paper was in easy-to-use rolls was not enough to get

Three different kinds of toilet paper sold in the nineteenth century—Silver Silk, India White Silk Tissue, and Victoria Single Fold

Toilet papers for sale by Montgomery Ward & Co. in its 1895 catalog

Some of the early brands following ScotTissue had great names, like Silver Silk, "The Aristocrat of Toilet Paper"; India White Silk Tissue, and Honest Count, guaranteed to contain 1,000 sheets in every roll.

Only 30 percent of the world's people use toilet paper; the rest must get by with alternatives, such as hands and water, rags, leaves, wastepaper, and other such items. Most unusual of all, in some parts of Africa and Asia, a wet rope is used for cleaning oneself.

A man in Japan has invented a toilet paper dispenser that attaches to a person's head! For a bad case of the sniffles, help is always at hand.

shoppers to put their money on the counter. Like Joseph Gayetty before him, Walter Alcock was soon out of business.

A year later, Irvin and Clarence Scott of Philadelphia introduced their own brand of perforated toilet tissue rolls. Because they faced the same problems as their predecessors, they sold their product at a very low price; also, so as "not to offend the public," the product went unnamed and was discreetly sold in plain brown wrappers. Later, tossing discretion to the wind, they put a name on the package: Waldorf Tissue, later ScotTissue (now spelled Scott Tissue).

The brand went over extremely well. Quality and price were two reasons; another was that indoor plumbing was becoming increasingly common. Many new homes, and most hotels, were being built with sinks, showers, and toilets. People began putting a roll of toilet paper next to the toilet. It was more sanitary—and more pleasant—than a stack of old newspapers and corncobs!

42 Toothbrush and Toothpaste

It's sort of hard to picture the early Egyptians—thousands of years ago—brushing their teeth. But they did. For a toothbrush, they used a "chew stick," a pencil-sized twig with one end frayed to a soft, bristlelike condition. For toothpaste, they used a concoction of vinegar and powdered pumice (a soft, crumbly volcanic stone).

Chew sticks are still used in remote parts of America and Africa. In Africa, twigs are taken from a tree called the *Salvadore persica*, or "toothbrush tree."

The Romans used chew sticks, too. And though it sounds totally disgusting, their toothpaste was human urine! They also used urine as a mouthwash. Roman doctors of the first century A.D. believed that this whitened teeth and fixed them more firmly in the gums.

The first bristle toothbrush was invented in China around 1498. The bristles were taken from the backs of the necks of hogs, horses, and badgers. Such toothbrushes reached Europe in the early 1700s, but they remained generally unknown and

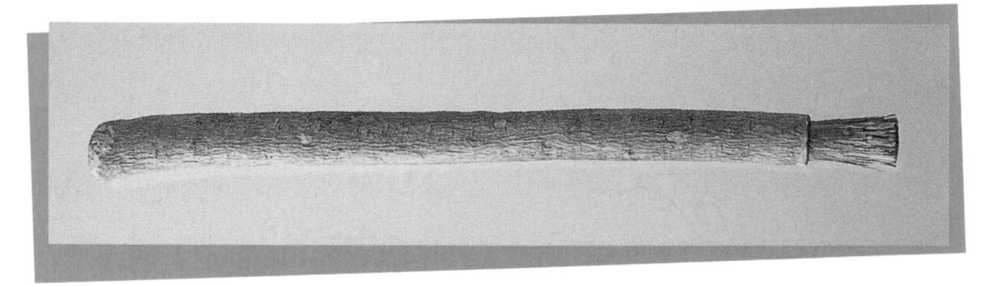

"Toothbrush twigs" were used by a great many cultures of the past—and are still used by a few today.

unused until a prisoner in an English jail, William Addis, reinvented and popularized them.

One morning in 1770, Addis, in his cell, was cleaning his teeth in the way most English people had for centuries—rubbing them with a rag. As he did, he wondered if he could make a toothbrush on the order of the Chinese devices he had heard about. He found a small piece of bone and a hairbrush. He bored tiny holes in one end of the bone, cut some bristles down to size, wedged them through the holes, and glued them in place. When he was done, he had a toothbrush in hand. Soon after being released from prison, Addis went into the toothbrush-making business. It flourished, and Addis was soon a wealthy, honest man.

Urine, as an active component in toothpastes and mouthwashes, continued to be used into the eighteenth century. Incidentally, urine *does* contain natural cleansing and whitening chemicals.

Until this time, toothpaste of any kind was basically nonexistent in Europe. A person could, however, go to what was called a barber-surgeon to have his or her teeth whitened. First, the barber-surgeon would file the patient's teeth with a coarse metal instrument, then dab them with aquafortis, a solution of highly corrosive nitric acid. The procedure produced brilliantly white teeth for a while, but over a period of a few short years, it also completely destroyed the enamel, causing massive dental decay.

Shortly after Addis popularized the toothbrush, people began concocting various toothpastes and powders. Most of these used baking

soda as the basic ingredient and came in small, round pots. In 1892, Dr. Washington Sheffield, an American dentist, invented the collapsible metal toothpaste tube. In 1953, the collapsible polyethylene (soft-plastic) tube was invented. A brand of skin-tanning lotion was the first product to be sold in this type of container; however, toothpaste was not far behind.

Under the name Dr. West's Miracle Tuft Toothbrush, the nylon-bristle brush was invented in 1938. The first electric toothbrush, the Broxodent, was introduced in 1961. A battery-operated, cordless model soon followed, as did a wide variety of new dental hygiene devices. One of those presently in the planning stages brings everything together: it consists of an electric brush with a slot for disposable cartridges of whiteners, washes, and pastes.

By the 1840s, in both Italy and France, dentists were recommending that people, from an early age, suck regularly on lozenges made with fluoride and sweetened with honey. Fluoride is a chemical that many people believe reduces cavities. It is found in some brands of toothpaste; and in communities where voters have approved the practice, it is added to the drinking water.

In the nineteenth century, Americans and others used tooth powders more than pastes. Cadette Tooth Powder For Children was one of the better sellers of the era; kids wanted the tin soldier as a toy when they used up the powder.

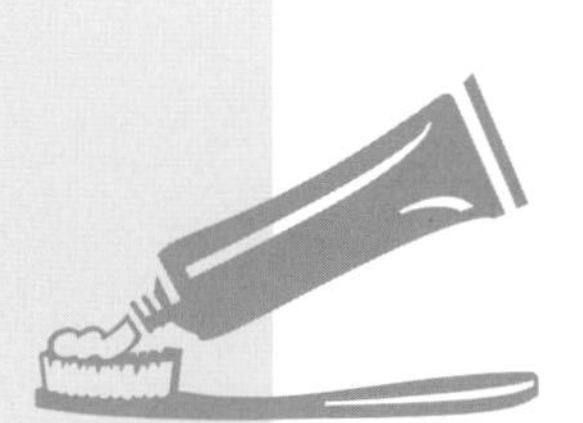

Trampoline

43

It all started with an eleven-year-old from Iowa named George Nissen. One day in 1926, George was at the circus with his family, watching tightrope walkers and trapeze artists. He thought they were great, especially when they intentionally took flying leaps to the safety net below—and then continued performing. They bounced up and down on the net and did twists, spins, and long, fantastic somersaults.

That's when the idea was born. When he was in high school, George decided he was going to make a device that would work like the safety net. It would be a small version that he and his friends could have fun jumping around on.

Before the trampoline, there was the "tossing blanket" of medieval Europe. With several people holding the edges of a large blanket, a person was tossed up and down in the air.

Soon George had taken over the family garage and begun work on what he called his "bouncing table." "Bouncing tables" had been made before, but mostly as props for stunts at carnivals and shows. What George wanted was a contraption that anyone could order for a backyard or gymnasium.

At the local junkyard, he hunted for materials—springs, rubber inner tubes, and metal for making a frame. Then he took his savings and bought a heavy-duty industrial sewing machine that could sew canvas.

All through high school and then through college, George

Circus horse walking a tightrope far above a safety net. The net was the inspiration for eleven-year-old George Nissen to invent—and eventually to manufacture and sell—trampolines.

In 1964, a "spaceball" fad swept the country. Spaceball is a sport combining elements of basketball and volleyball and played on a trampoline. In that same year, the International Trampoline Federation was formed with seven member nations. Today over forty nations are members, and, for the first time ever, trampolining was a medal sport at the Olympics in Sydney, Australia, in September 2000.

kept working on his invention. He and his friends had a good time clowning around on the thing. But George was always looking for ways to improve it. It had to be safe, have great bounce, and be strong enough to withstand all kinds of jumping. It was also important that it be easy to transport, set up, and store.

It took almost twelve years. But finally, in 1937, George had created a "bouncing table" that met most of his requirements. He had also invented the machines necessary to produce them and had changed the name to *trampoline*, from the Spanish word *trampolín*, meaning "springboard."

He was now ready, he decided, to make his fame and fortune selling his invention. With trampolines strapped to the top of his old car, he set off on a cross-country tour. In town after town, he demonstrated his contraption in any place where there would be crowds—in front of supermarkets, at parks, at county fairs, and outside sports stadiums. With the money he made from these exhibitions, he bought more materials and continued to develop and improve his invention.

During World War II, George enlisted in the U.S. Navy. Before long, he had persuaded both the army and navy to use trampolines in their preflight training programs, especially those for soldiers learning to be paratroopers and pilots.

In 1981, Jeff Schwartz of Illinois set the record for bouncing on a trampoline the longest. Schwartz bounced for 266 hours, 9 minutes—a period of more than eleven days. (The rules allowed him closely clocked time-outs for eating, sleeping, and using the rest room.)

After the war, George went into the trampoline business full-time. Sales were slow at first, but then they suddenly skyrocketed. George's hard work, persistence, and unflagging optimism had finally paid off. People bought trampolines for their backyards. Colleges added them to their gymnastics programs. NASA began using them to give astronauts the feeling of weightlessness that the trampoline simulates.

And there's another place where you're bound to see the invention. It's the place where a kid first got the idea for them: at the circus.

During a promotional tour in Europe, George Nissen used a kangaroo to prove that users of his bouncy invention could outjump it. He kept a supply of dried apricots as treats to encourage the kangaroo to cooperate. He also learned that by holding its front paws, he could avoid being kicked!

44

Vacuum Cleaner

During the 1800s, many people tried to invent the vacuum cleaner. There were neither electric cords on these early devices nor any wall sockets to plug into. Instead of electricity, most of the contraptions used bellows to create airflow. Some were operated by hand, some by foot, and one by the wheels of the sweeper. This last type was the most clever. As the machine was pulled across the floor, the turning of its wheels caused the bellows to open and close.

Prior to developing his vacuum cleaner, Hubert Booth built bridges and Ferris wheels.

Instead of sucking air in, almost all of these early vacuum cleaners blew air out. Dust and dirt went flying. Clouds of the stuff hovered in the air, then gradually just settled back down again on carpeting and furniture.

One day in 1901, Englishman Hubert Booth and some friends watched as a team of workers attempted to clean the interior of a train car. As usual, the results were laughably unsatisfactory. Later, at a restaurant with his friends, Booth declared that vacuum cleaners had to be made to suck air in, not blow it out. Some sort of filtration device was also needed, he told them. To demonstrate his point, Booth placed a handkerchief over the back of a plush chair, put his lips to it, and sucked. A dirty black oval appeared on the handkerchief.

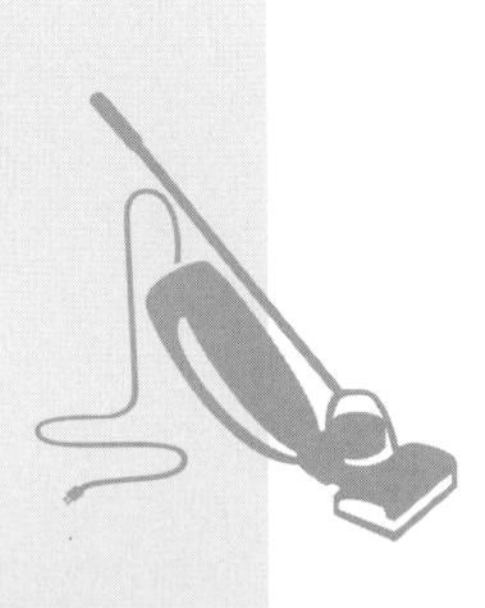

This enormous vacuum—the "mobile office cleaner"—was pulled by a horse through the streets. Long hoses attached to the suction machine on the cart were stretched into houses and other buildings.

It took Booth almost a year, but finally he succeeded in constructing the world's first truly effective vacuum cleaner. A gas-powered motor pulled air in, and a baglike cloth filter collected the dust. When the bag was full, it could be removed and replaced.

Booth's vacuum worked extremely well. The only problem with it was its size. It was a huge thing—about the size of a refrigerator—and weighed several hundred pounds! For this reason, instead of trying to sell his invention, Booth started a cleaning service. The vacuum was mounted on a horse-drawn van, which brought it to the customer's house. Then, with 800-foot-long hoses snaking through open windows, the operator cleaned the dirt from carpeting, drapes, and furniture.

Booth was often in trouble with the police because the gas-powered motor utilized by his huge, horse-drawn vacuum cleaner was incredibly noisy.

Within a few years, smaller, portable vacuum cleaners were being produced for home use. Since many people did not yet have electricity in their homes, most of these vacuums were operated manually. In 1905, a company in San Francisco introduced a model that was mounted on a trolley, with suction being created by pumping a large handle. A bit stranger was the Kotten Suction Sweeper, introduced a few years later. A person had to stand on top of the thing and rock from side to side in order to produce suction. Vacuum cleaners such as these usually required at least two people to operate them: one to crank or pedal the bellows, the other to apply the nozzle to

The Regina Company, which made one of the best of the early models for home use, began as the Regina Music Box Company.

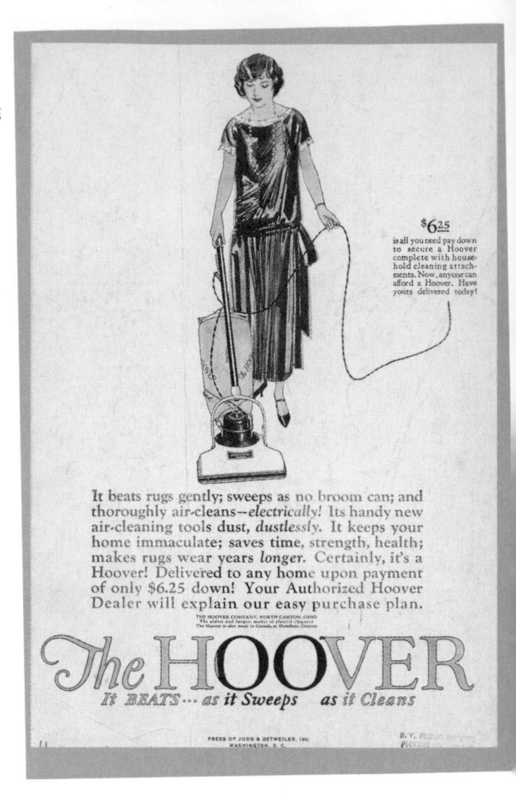

A Hoover ad from 1924

the floor and furnishings.

In 1907, James Spangler, a janitor in an Ohio department store, had an idea. Using a broom handle, pillowcase, and the motor from an electric fan, he invented the upright vacuum cleaner. At first, his only real purpose in creating this truly ingenious device was to make his job a bit easier; it enabled him to stand upright when vacuuming, thus taking a great deal of strain off his back. Then he began to wonder if he might make some money from his invention.

One early vacuum had a water-filled container inside it for filtering out dust. Some of the high-end models today use this same filtration method.

Spangler showed his upright vacuum to a childhood friend, William Hoover. Hoover purchased the patent and then formed a new company. Spangler was in charge of production, and Hoover handled the business end of the venture.

On average, vacuum cleaners last for eight years.

The company was a success from the start. By the mid-1920s, the brand had become so well known that people referred to vacuuming as "Hoovering." To this day, people in England still use this term.

One of William Hoover's sales techniques was sending teams of salesmen from house to house to demonstrate the product. When the door opened, the salesmen sang "The Hoover Song": *All the dirt, all the grit/Hoover gets it, every bit.*

Pretty lame stuff, but a lot of vacuum cleaners were sold in this way. All it took was a good product and a salesman willing to sing a really embarrassing song.

Vaseline®
(petroleum jelly)

In 1859, a young chemist named Robert Chesebrough traveled from New York to Pennsylvania, where he hoped to get a job in the oil business. In the Pennsylvania oil fields, he found that the workers constantly complained about a pasty, waxlike residue that clogged pumps and gummed up drilling rods. The only good thing about the stuff, said the workers, was that it could be rubbed on burns and cuts to ease the pain and speed up healing. Intrigued, Chesebrough returned to New York with jars of the strange petroleum waste product. After months of experimentation, he was able to extract and purify the paste's basic ingredient to create a clear, smooth substance he called "petroleum jelly." Using himself as a guinea pig, he inflicted small cuts, scratches, and burns on his arms and legs, then applied the substance to test its effectiveness.

To promote his product, Chesebrough traveled the roads of New York State, giving away free jars of the gooey salve to anyone who promised to try it on a cut or burn.

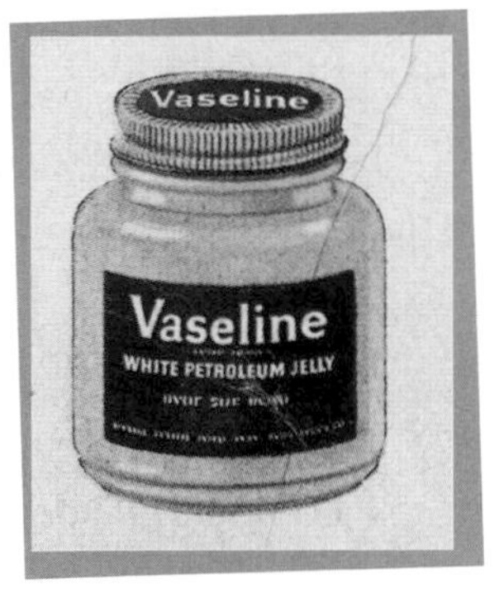

By 1870, Chesebrough was manufacturing petroleum jelly and selling it under the name Vaseline. He called it that because, in his early days of experimentation, he had used his wife's flower vases as laboratory beakers. To *vase* he

A 1953 ad for Vaseline hair tonic

Chesebrough, who lived to the age of ninety-six, attributed his longevity to Vaseline petroleum jelly: he ate a spoonful of it every day!

Before a football game in 1986, players on the Citadel Bulldogs team smeared their bodies and jerseys with petroleum jelly to make themselves harder to tackle. All to no avail. The greasy Bulldogs lost, 27–12.

tagged on a popular medicinal suffix of the day, *line*.

Petroleum jelly is the base component of many modern brands of salves, creams, and cosmetics. Other uses: Farmers slather it on outdoor machinery to keep the metal parts from rusting; baseball players use it to soften their gloves; long-distance swimmers smear it on their bodies to retain heat; actors even use it to simulate perspiration! Smeared on their skin, it makes them look lustrously sweaty.

Vending Machine

The vending machine is full of surprises.

The first vending machine (invented by a man named Hero of Alexandria) dispensed holy water. The device, made of copper, was installed in a Greek temple in Egypt in 213 B.C. When a coin was dropped through a slot, its weight briefly opened a spigot, releasing a trickle of priest-blessed water. Worshipers would wet their hands and touch the water to their heads.

Vending machines next popped up in England in 1615 (in Shakespeare's time). Inserting a penny into a slot opened the lock on a box filled with pipe tobacco. They were called "honesty boxes," because the customer was on his honor to take no more than a pipeful, the permissible limit.

In some Japanese cities, there are vending machines that offer "hits" of pure oxygen.

The first *automatic* vending machine did not appear until 1867. Invented by Carl Ade of Germany, it dispensed handkerchiefs, cigarettes, and candy. Only one machine was made, and it's not known for sure if it was ever actually put into operation.

In 1883, Percival Everitt of England invented the first workable and commercially successful automatic vending machine. Set against the back wall of a platform at a railway station, it dispensed postcards. It was soon turning a profit—but much of that was offset by vandalism. A distressed Everitt wrote:

"Although the apparatus is perfectly successful when not designedly misused, articles such as paper, orange peel, and other rubbish have been maliciously placed in the slot provided for the admission of the coin."

Because of vandalism, Everitt almost called it quits. But then he appealed to the British Parliament. Soon a law was passed protecting vending machines from vandals. Everitt was back in business.

By 1887, Everitt had adapted vending machines to dispense a wide range of items. Goods available at the drop of a coin included eggs, biscuits, cologne, condensed milk, sugar, cough drops, and accident insurance.

The spread of automatic vending to other countries followed rapidly. Early in 1888, the English machines were being used in the United States. Before year's end, U.S. inventors were making their own machines, adapting them to all sorts of new uses.

The Dial-A-Sale (of the 1960s) was the world's largest-ever vending machine. This monster was nine feet high and five feet deep. Offering up to 204 different items, the thing was designed to be an entire department store.

Chewing gum was the first thing sold in this country from a U.S.-made machine. Slot machines (for gambling) appeared next, in 1889; peanut-vending came out two years later. Then things got weird. In 1895, the citizens of Corinne, Utah, found they were able to obtain divorce papers quickly, easily, and automatically—from a vending machine! The cost: $2.50. Just fill out the papers, sign on the dotted line, and you're unhitched.

Other countries also had their own outrageous machines.

In 1924 in Berlin, Germany, a machine went into operation that dispensed a college diploma. For the equivalent of one dollar, you could get a paper to hang on the wall that made others think that you were a college graduate.

Food has long been a vending-machine mainstay. At first, you could get just a few basic items—sugar, milk, bread, et cetera. In 1961, an American inventor decided that what the world needed was an all-vending-machine supermarket. Calling it the Food-O-Matic, this genius further decided to have it built into the storefront of a regular market.

"Stupidest thing I've ever seen," a woman told a reporter after seeing the place on opening day. "Who's going to buy food from a machine when they can walk right into the store and get the same thing?"

The Food-O-Matic was out of business in a matter of months. A semi-fancy, all-vending-machine restaurant that offered hot items fell flat on its face the same year.

Toothbrushes, soap, shower caps, towels, and other per-

Hugo Gernsback predicted umbrella-vending machines in his little-known sci-fi novel *Ein Pecvogel.*

If you decide to use a vending machine in Japan, don't be surprised if beetles are among the items that come out. Beetle collecting is a popular pastime in Japan.

The 1961 Food-O-Matic was a coin-operated vending-machine grocery store built into the front of a grocery store! Seemed like a great idea at the time, but it was an immediate flop. Not enough people used the machines even to pay for the constant repairs they needed.

The Book-O-Mat was another vending failure of the 1960s.

The first novel sold through vending machines was Agatha Christie's *Murder on the Orient Express.*

In Paris, France, there are vending machines from which you can purchase Levi's. Each machine has a seat belt you strap around your waist to determine your size.

In Spain, the fast-food company Telepizza makes a machine that attracts (or repels?) customers by shouting, "Hey, want a pizza?" in ten languages.

sonal-hygiene products have become increasingly popular since the early 1950s. Sunscreen is now sold in packets, but when it first hit the market, it splurted out of a nozzle. For a time, you could even get a shave from one unique vending machine. In the early 1960s, for a quarter, the machine let you use a Norelco electric shaver. When you were done, you got a squirt of aftershave.

Clothing has been coming out of vending machines from the beginning. At first, it was hankies and socks. Over the years, all sorts of other articles of clothing became available—neckties, gloves, swim trunks, raincoats, pajamas, and T-shirts, just to name a few. Funniest of all, in the summer of 1960, a men's-underwear vending machine was unveiled at a Macy's department store in Chicago. It caused such a sensation it was on the national news. People hurried to the store in droves—but not to get underpants, just a good laugh.

Videotape

47

Today almost all TV shows are taped. But before the invention of videotaping, TV shows were broadcast live—which meant that audiences saw all sorts of crazy bloopers and blunders. During one show in 1952, a comedian was changing his clothes between skits. The curtain opened a little too soon, and the man ended up onstage (and on national TV) without any pants or underwear on!

Invented in 1951, the first audiovisual recorder was about as big as a stove and weighed over 1,200 pounds. To get just a few minutes of playback, it needed literally thousands of feet of tape. As for the quality, it was atrocious—especially the video part. The picture was just a fuzzy blur. There was also a problem with the sound: it was almost always out of sync with the picture.

In 1952, Charles Ginsburg, a scientist at the Ampex Company, in Redlands, California, was put in charge of finding a way to improve audio-video recorders. After a few months, he thought he had made a good deal of progress—enough to put on a demonstration for the president of the company. Ginsburg taped a cowboy movie, then played it for his boss. As the two watched a flickering collage of shadows, Ginsburg's face

The scientific team that Ginsburg headed at the Ampex Company included a college student named Ray Dolby, who went on to develop the famous Dolby Sound System.

Ginsburg's recording system was used commercially for the first time on November 30, 1956. CBS taped *Douglas Edwards with the News* when it was broadcast in New York. The program was replayed three hours later on the West Coast.

turned bright red with embarrassment. "Wonderful!" exclaimed the president sarcastically. "Wonderful movie! But which one is the cowboy and which one is the horse?"

Ginsburg wanted to crawl under his desk and hide. Instead, he just apologized to his boss and went back to work, trying to figure out what had gone wrong and how he might fix it.

For four long years, he and his staff experimented with different approaches to bettering the equipment. Finally, they were pretty sure they had identified what was causing all the problems with both the picture and the sound. Another demonstration was arranged for the morning of February 5,

Invented in 1967, the first "instant replay" system for sports used a large metal disc to record the action. Although it could record only thirty seconds of programming at a time, a desired bit of footage could be located and readied for replay in less than four seconds.

Look at the size of this 1951 VCR! A VCR today is the size of a small briefcase, and they're getting smaller all the time.

1956. Not only would the president be there; so would all the employees of the company.

In his diary, Ginsburg described what happened:

"The guests—about thirty, or so—arrived, and took seats in the main conference room. . . . I then announced that we would make a recording of what was on TV and then immediately play it back. . . . I recorded for about two minutes, then rewound and stopped the tape. Every eye in the room was on the TV screen—waiting to see what would happen. My hand shaking, I pushed the playback button. The show I'd recorded began replaying, and looked as good and clear as it had the first time! Completely silent up to this point, the entire group suddenly rose to its feet; the building shook with applause and shouting. I was thrilled, ecstatic. I shook hands with my colleagues, my staff. 'We did it!' I yelled happily."

In 1978 at a Doncaster, England, department store, police set up a surveillance camera to catch a thief who had been swiping clothes out of the changing rooms. At day's end, when the police played back the recording, what they had caught on tape was one of their own policemen wandering around naked and looking for his clothes, which had been stolen.

In 1995, a woman in Virginia forgot to return four videotapes and was almost three months overdue in bringing them back to the store where she had rented them. The woman was arrested, and the judge ordered her to pay a fine of $400 to the store and to stand trial for her "crime"—punishable by up to one year in jail!

Because of surveillance cameras, it is estimated that you are on camera more than 80 percent of the time when you are shopping.

48 Water Hose

The earliest flexible hose dates from as early as 7 B.C. and was made from the intestines of animals. Human intestinal tracts are twenty-five to thirty feet long; those of large mammals such as horses, cows, and elephants are many times longer. After being cleaned and dried, such hoses were reasonably sturdy. Their purpose, as it is today, was to get water from one place to another.

The Bible mentions "water skins." Used for carrying water, they were made from animal stomachs. In making them, part of the small intestine and esophagus were left intact, which created flexible hoses for filling and pouring.

The ancient Romans used hoses made of leather, as did the Minoans, another Mediterranean civilization (5000 to 1200 B.C.). These hoses were made of leather strips wound in a spiral and bound with leather thongs. Such hoses were used in the elaborate plumbing systems of Minoa.

Amazingly, leather hoses were the only kind available for the next six thousand years! Not until the nineteenth century was the rubber hose invented.

One day in 1870, Dr. Benjamin

A fireman using a cotton-covered Goodrich fire hose

Goodrich, a former Civil War surgeon, was in his backyard in Akron, Ohio. He smelled smoke and heard a commotion not far away. He hurried down the street to find that a fire had broken out in the house of one of his neighbors. Bell clanging, hooves pounding, a horse-drawn fire truck raced to the scene. Immediately, a large leather fire hose was connected to the pumper spigot and unrolled. The hose swelled as it filled with water; it began to leak, then suddenly burst. As a result, the house burned to the ground.

The *B.F.* in B.F. Goodrich stands for Benjamin Franklin.

Right then and there, Goodrich decided that leather hoses had to go. Leather is not very elastic. When repeatedly wet and dried, it ages, becomes brittle, and easily cracks or ruptures.

At the time of the fire, Goodrich already owned and ran a factory for making rubber goods (including rubber tires, for which he is best known). Within a few months of the blaze that took his neighbor's home, he was producing the world's first fire hoses. The heavy-duty, cotton-covered rubber hoses quickly became Goodrich's best-selling product. Smaller, lightweight rubber garden hoses soon followed.

In the early 1970s, an Englishman by the name of Arthur Pedrick patented the idea of irrigating the deserts of the world by sending a constant supply of snowballs from polar regions through a giant network of plastic hoses!

During World War II, synthetic rubber was invented. One of its first peacetime uses was for hoses. The war also saw the development of many new types of plastic, some of which were flexible. By the 1950s, Americans were watering their lawns with plastic hoses as well as those made from natural and synthetic rubber.

Windsurfer™

Newman Darby made his first attempt to build a boat while in middle school. It sank, but he never gave up—and went on to become quite an inventor!

Photographers and writers for *Popular Science* were blown away by the Darbys' sailboard when they saw Naomi's younger sister, who was only sixteen at the time, catch a particularly good breeze—and outpace a motorboat on the water! On a Windsurfer, you can shoot along the surface of the water at speeds of up to forty-five knots (fifty-two miles per hour)!

Three thousand years ago, native people living along the Amazon River sailed on raftlike boards with movable masts. Such boards were up to twenty feet long and could carry many passengers. The men and women fished from them—and used them as an integral part of their daily life.

Boards of this kind next pop up on a beach in Southern California in the 1930s, in the earliest days of the surfing craze there. One day a surfer named Tom Blake was exhausted from paddling his board out to catch waves. He dreamed of how great it would be to use the wind for propulsion. At home, he went to work on making the idea a reality. Blake added a mast to his surfboard, and even devised a foot-controlled rudder to what he called his "sailing surfboard." It worked well, but Blake never really tried very hard to manufacture and market his creation. Mostly it was just for his own enjoyment and that of his family and friends.

Thirty years later, in the 1960s, Newman and Naomi Darby came up with the idea of the sailboard. Unlike Blake's invention, it was designed more for sailing than surfing. An article about the Darbys' invention was published in *Popular Science* magazine in 1965.

Even before they were married, inventors Newman and Naomi Darby were experimenting with sailboards. This 1964 photo of Naomi is the earliest known photograph of anyone using a free-sail system.

In 1966, three friends were sitting around talking on a beach in Southern California. Jim Drake, Hoyle Schweitzer, and Allen Parducci were surfers, and all three liked sailing. They decided that somehow they would design a sailboard that a person could ride standing up, like a surfboard. It would be for their own enjoyment, but it might be a great business product, too!

They called their invention the Baja Board. Like the Darbys' sailboard, the Baja Board had a "universal joint," which allowed the mast, boom, and sail assembly to move in all directions. In addition, there were foot straps and a seat harness to give the rider more stability and control. A "dagger board," a small rectangular fin that was pushed down through a slot into the water, kept the board moving straight ahead.

Windsurfing became an Olympic sport at the 1984 Los Angeles Games.

In 1969, Hoyle Schweitzer started a business that he called Windsurfer. Then he began traveling around the country, promoting the sport and his board. In 1971, the sport was introduced in Europe, where it became an immediate success.

Today there are many brands of boards. In ordinary speech, one brand name, as often happens, became the name of the sport: windsurfing.

50

Zamboni®
(ice resurfacer)

The first ice skates were made of polished animal bones attached to leather boots.

Ice skates as we know them today—boots with metal blades—were invented in the 1870s by Jackson Haines, an American figure skater.

Back in the early 1930s, in Paramount, California, teenagers Frank Zamboni and his brother Lawrence were "ice men." Using what little money they had, the two built a small refrigeration plant and sold blocks of ice to local farmers and townspeople for their "ice boxes"— large, insulated wooden chests. Then, in the 1940s, the electrical refrigerator began destroying the market for home-delivered ice. The brothers knew they would soon be out of business.

But instead of giving up, the Zambonis decided to build an ice-skating rink. In 1940, a few blocks from their ice-making plant, they opened the Iceland Skating Rink to the public.

Business was good, but keeping the place going was hard work, especially cleaning and resurfacing the ice every night. The process included mopping up dirty water, scraping and smoothing the old ice, then hauling off the scrapings and other debris. Finally, using an extra-long garden hose, they spread a fresh layer of water, which soon froze, leaving a new, smooth surface of ice. Three or four workers were needed, and from start to finish, the job took up to two hours to complete.

In 1942, the Zamboni brothers bought an old Jeep and began experimenting with ways to mechanize the ice-resurfacing process. Gradually they added all sorts of new features and devices to the vehicle—and by 1949 had created a huge, lumbering contraption. Although it was weird-looking, the thing worked beautifully. It scraped the ice, scooped up the residue, squeegeed the surface, and spread a nice, even coat of water—all in a period of fifteen minutes for the entire rink.

Iceland Skating Rink is still in business. In fact, it is one of the largest rinks in the country, with 20,000 square feet of iced surface. That's enough for 800 skaters!

One of the boys' customers was Olympic medalist and Hollywood skating star Sonja Henie, who rented practice time at the Iceland rink for herself and members of her touring group. When she saw the Zamboni brothers' machine in action, she ordered two to take along on her annual national tour—inadvertently giving their creation great coast-to-coast advertising. Soon orders for the machines were pouring in from ice-

Olympic skating star Sonja Henie in front of her Zamboni® ice resurfacer. Ms. Henie ordered the second and third of these machines ever sold.

XING

arena managers all across the country. International exposure came in 1960 when the ice resurfacers were used during the Winter Olympics at Squaw Valley, California.

Today the Zambonis' invention is used in almost forty countries. Each new machine produced goes through an interesting, ceremonial sort of ritual. First, it is test-driven down the main street of the town of Paramount. Then, upon reaching the Iceland Skating Rink, it is taken for a few turns around the rink before being driven off toward the railroad station for shipping.

Iceland was originally an open-air facility. But the brothers soon learned that the hot, dry Southern California climate often ruined the quality of the ice, so they covered it with a domed roof.

To create an Olympic skating rink of 185 by 85 feet, approximately ten miles of pipe are laid out crosswise on a cement floor. The rink is then flooded with about three inches of water, and a freezing solution running through the pipes turns the water to ice.